RAYNE STORM

RAYNE STORM

JOHN B. THOMPSON

CUTTING EDGE

ISBN-13: 978-1-954840-66-9

Published by
Cutting Edge Books
PO Box 8212
Calabasas, CA 91372
www.cuttingedgebooks.com

CHAPTER ONE

ACROSS THE DESK from Rayne Cantey, his recent employer smiled, but even the sweetest smile could achieve little toward softening the intelligent strength of that powerful face. It was too strong, the eyes were too steady, and the jaw too square and truculent.

"I'm going to change the rules, Rayne. The next fledgling operative I interview, I'm going to inquire about rich relatives. And if he has any I'm going to terminate the interview right there. I lose too many good men to the lure of the dollar."

"You make me sound like a tycoon," said Rayne, returning the smile.

"Maybe not a tycoon, but you have enough soaked away and enough coming in to make what I pay small change. I'll be sorry to lose you and I think you know that. There was a time when I could run a question through my mechanical brain and come up with a name that could answer anything I wanted to know about any town over five hundred population anywhere in the world. Not any more. Too much side-taking now. So I get a lot of colored information and I don't want anything but the cold facts. In you I had the Near and Far East on hand. With you gone the quality of my information will suffer. I won't like that."

"I told you I'd help out anytime I could."

"Sure. Ellis Kronk said the same thing. Know where he is?"

"In Lebanon or Iraq or some place."

"Right. He was in Israel the last time they kicked hell out of Nasser. But what good is he to me?"

"Well, I won't be there. I'll be plantationing in Louisiana. I'll hunt the enemy when I'm asked, not before. I'm no soldier of fortune."

"What will you do?"

"Nothing. Watch my cattle and play with a breed I like. *Santa Gertrudis.* They were developed on the King Ranch in Texas."

"You'd better do something. I've found that men who are built like you with lean tense faces don't do very well sitting."

"What's wrong with my build and my face?"

"Nothing. You walk like you're about to leap on someone. You make me think of a fused triton block." He laughed and tapped the bulky folder before him. "The records bear me out. Why don't you learn to relax?"

"I can, but I have to have everything right. I'll be able to relax on the plantation."

Maybe. Rayne, do you think of yourself as a brave man?"

"No."

The thickset man leaned back in his chair and lit a stumpy pipe that strangely resembled him.

"I'm glad you said that. Tell me about it."

"Nothing to tell and since you're enough of a psychologist to know the etiology of fear—"

"Of course, I know all that." He patted the folder again. "In here are some incidents that have made me wonder."

"You mean blasting that Ellery mob?"

"Well, yes. The Ellery mob, Layton Dodge and his two brothers—things like that."

Rayne sat on the edge of his chair and tapped the padded surface of the big desk. "Ed, it's like this. In the case of the Ellery fracas, I was by myself, surrounded, and in possession of some things they'd have given their right arms, all of them, to get. I was scared stiff because they were hardened murderers and they'd have snuffed me out like a light. I did the only thing I could with the circumstances as they were. I know it would have been a lot better if I had brought them in but in my considered opinion, I couldn't have done it. I love my country but I love me too."

The other nodded. "Mind you, I'm not blaming you. No one is. But in reading this over I said to myself, 'Rayne'll tackle a swarm of wildcats single-handed and knock off every last one of them.'"

Rayne shrugged. "Your guess was right. When I get in an impossible spot I'm scared to death. When I'm scared I'm likely to try to blast my way out. I keep remembering men like White, Caldwell and Bergin. All dead as mackerel and six feet under because they tried to be decent to a soulless criminal. Bergin let DeFerrest go in another room to tell his wife goodbye and paid for being white with his life. Caldwell didn't think a little puff like. Lena Harpe was anything but a spoiled brat and for that he got a shiv in his aorta. That's the way it goes. When I have the drop and the situation well in hand, well and good. But when I know I'm being dealt a hand from a cold deck, I get scared."

The older man nodded. "Let's drop it. As I say, I have no criticism because I know why you act as you do. I can sit here and give orders to anybody, but put me in a spot like the one you were in and I'd probably be twice as scared and three times as quick to shoot. Well, no matter. We'll be sorry to lose you, but before you go I have something for you."

He handed Rayne a little white card encased in stiff plastic.

Rayne read it carefully and turned it over. He whistled softly. "I've seen just one of these."

"Who? Norcross?"

"Yes. Tell me, how do you decide who gets these?"

"By one of the toughest screening tests ever devised, and even then they aren't thrown around. The qualifications are too tough."

"Mind telling me what they are? And when was I screened?"

"I'll tell you a few. First, there must be a certain type of personality. You and Norcross have it. In fact, you're a lot alike. Your screening? That started the day you went to work for me."

"I see. I always looked upon Norcross as a man who had even less compunction than me."

"There are twenty of those cards in circulation and, oddly enough, when you get home there will be three in your state alone."

"Do you attach any significance to that?"

"Not particularly, except that for some reason a lot of people come from down there who fit. There are two on the west coast, two in New York, three in Britain, two in Texas with a good six more possibles down there. The other eight are scattered around. Canada has a couple, South Africa, India, Australia and oddly enough, one in Tutuila, American Samoa. He's half native but a graduate of Annapolis. His war record, largely in the Philippines, isn't widely known. If it were, they'd have to give him the Congressional Medal."

"Get on with the qualifications."

"It isn't easy to tell you. We don't want men who kill for plea-sure and we don't want men who will run at the first sign of defeat. The only reason we issue this card is because that little thing can get you cooperation from any police force in any friendly nation and it gives us a nucleus of men to work with should there be any sudden international emergency. With these twenty men, there would be a force of armed men I could trust in three days, a force over fifty thousand strong. Isn't that right?"

Rayne's brow furrowed with concentration, then he smiled. "Well, I'll be damned. For a moment there I was ready to say I couldn't help that much from my end—but hell, I could give you a couple thousand in twenty-four hours. Men you wouldn't have to waste a minute screening."

"And you could lead them, too."

Rayne shrugged. "Modesty forbids—"

"Modesty, my aching corn." He tapped the folder. "How many officers did the Second Marine Division lose on Saipan before you had command?"

Rayne blushed. "Oh, shut up. That was under pressure."

"If I ever call on you for anything other than a chore, son, you'll be under the sort of pressure you've never imagined."

Rayne Cantey sat on the porch of his house and watched with pride the thick-shouldered bull grazing on the meadow that extended half a mile in front of the house to the line of woods. He had the bull and three cows—that had cost him a tidy sum—and all three cows were in calf-producing condition. Six feet away sat Tom White, a neighbor and fellow *Santa Gertrudis* enthusiast.

"Your old man will turn in his grave, Ray. There ain't a white face cow on the place."

"Times change, Tom. I remember when he was just as strong for Red Polls."

"That's right." Tom was bean pole tall and rail thin, with no teeth and a freckling of tobacco juice on his white shirt front. Rayne had never seen him without a white shirt and a black string tie drooping amid the freckles.

"Amy 'lows as to how you ought to be married."

Rayne chuckled. "Me? Who'd marry me?"

"Just about any gal in the parish—if you'd give any of 'em a tumble."

"Well, I'm not in a tumbling mood."

"What sorta mood is you in?"

"I'm beginning to wonder myself. I came back here all ready to relax and raise cattle and damned if I'm not getting restless again."

"Well, one thing for sure—if you want action, you come to the wuss place in the world. The last thing what happened here was when them gypsies run off with Mack Peter's paint hoss."

Rayne scratched his chin ruminatively. "They used to say I was born for trouble."

"Who said that?"

"The fellows I used to work with. And you know, Tom, I can sort of feel it coming. As you say, though—what could happen here?"

"You could get bit by a cotton mouth or you could get your neck broke ridin' that hoss so damn hard. But I b'lieve you seen too many cowboy pictures when you was in Washington."

That night, with crickets sawing contentedly in the grass and toads rasping peacefully all around the house, Rayne himself began to wonder what could happen in such surroundings.

Was a wife what he needed? He shrugged hard with distaste. Of all the men he knew, he felt less equal to the constraining complications of marriage. The bare thought that he must knuckle under to vows, be home on time, and establish some kind of inflexible routine, made him cringe with revolt and even anger.

He had been home two months now; the house was relatively new, very comfortable, and everything else was arranged to provide for the least irritation. There shouldn't be a worry in his mind. But he had been conscious of a vague unrest and discomfort for the last few weeks. He lit a cigarette and watched how the moon changed to the color of the smoke as the wisps floated into its light. He was comfortable, his stomach was full of good food—he ate at the White's regularly and Amy stuffed him—and he could find nothing to which to ascribe his irritation—but there it was.

He went back into the house and made a tall drink of scotch, seltzer and ice, came back to the porch and sat down in his chair again. Hardly had he sat when Tater, his mongrel watchdog, ran from under the house, brushing the switch canes where they grew thickly close to the porch, making one of them snap sharply with a report like a small bore pistol.

Rayne came to his feet like a released spring, sweeping his hand past an armpit in sheer reflex motion. Then he realized what had caused the noise. He bit back a sudden acid blaze of anger, realizing that he was angry because he had been made to react hastily but without cause. Tater finished his reconnaissance and came back wagging his tail.

"Get the hell under there and stay there!" said Rayne ill-temperedly, feeling very foolish.

At the edge of the woods where boiler tubes had been laid over a pit to form a cattle guard, he saw the lights of a car. They glimmered on the worn surface of the tubes, then came into full view, bobbing and sweeping the pasture as the car went over the guard.

"Now who…" thought Rayne, smiling as he realized that every country person always thought or spoke the same words when the lights of a car were sighted at night.

As it came nearer, he saw that it was not a jalopy or one of the small cars used by most of his neighbors. He stared as it hissed to a stop in front of his gate because it was probably the first Rolls Royce ever seen in St. Louis Parish. His brow creased with a frown of curiosity as he rose to his feet and stood waiting at the steps as two men descended and came through the picket gate. As they came nearer, he could see that they were small, that they were dark—that they were Orientals.

The leader stopped at the steps and bowed politely. "Have I the honor to address Mr. Rayne Cantey?"

"You have, although the nature of the honor escapes me."

"I am K. J. Chaing and this is a friend, Mr. Kung."

"How do you do. Will you have chairs?"

"You are most kind," said Mr. Chaing and Mr. Kung bowed and hissed softly, but Rayne didn't catch the words.

"This is a visit I hardly anticipated, Mr. Chaing. I rather imagine that you're the first members of your country to honor our parish."

"I suspected as much when I asked directions, Mr. Cantey. I suppose it is rather odd to be visited at this hour by those you

7

least expect by virtue of your locality. I understand that there are some of my people in New Orleans."

"And New Orleans is a hundred and twenty miles away," said Rayne, smiling. "Since the visit obviously is not a social one, suppose you get to the real purpose of it."

"The Anglo-Saxons are so precipitous a people," hissed Mr. Kung.

Rayne nodded, somewhat irritated. "I suppose so. Maybe that's why they get things done."

Mr. Chaing cast a swift murderous look at Mr. Kung, then smiled at Rayne. "That is precisely why we are here. You have quite a reputation for getting things done."

"In what way may I be of service?" Rayne prodded, annoyed.

Mr. Chaing cleared his throat nervously. "The nature of my task makes beginning difficult."

"Your task? Or the one you hope to persuade me to accept?"

Mr. Chaing was obviously taken aback. "Is it possible that you have advance notice..."

"No. If you know of my reputation, then you must see that the possibilities are not unlimited. I was a government agent and I have certain talents. I assume that you wish to hire them."

"Precisely and shrewdly arrived at," enthused Mr. Chaing while Mr. Kung bowed and hissed between his buck teeth.

"You, Mr. Cantey," began Mr. Chaing pompously, "were recommended to me—"

"By whom?"

The other spread his hands. "Alas, I am sworn to secrecy. I am not at liberty to reveal the source of my information."

Rayne's eyes narrowed. "Go on."

"You were recommended as a brave and resourceful man, one who would suit our purposes admirably, if not to say perfectly."

"And what are your purposes?"

Mr. Chaing looked around. "You are alone here, Mr. Cantey?"

"I have a dog, a horse, and several cattle. They're not interested."

"Ah, so." He smiled and folded his hands in his lap. "We, Mr. Cantey, are patriots and are the representatives of a patriotic organization …"

"Whose purpose is what?" asked Rayne bluntly.

Mr. Chaing's oblique eyebrows went up. "Why, to restore to our prostrate country her rightful and legal government."

"Deciding that alone should be a job in itself—but continue," commented Rayne drily.

"Therefore, we are interested—we are anxious to recover some property of the Kuomintang Government and restore it to the safe-keeping of the Generalissimo. You, Mr. Cantey, we hope to persuade to recover it."

"And how would you describe this property?"

"It is a lacquered steel box, ten inches long and five inches wide."

"And in the box?"

"That will not concern you. Upon recovery you will, with all haste, and the utmost caution, deliver it to me."

"What do I get out of the venture?"

"The day you deliver me the box you will receive twenty thousand dollars cash. I am prepared to advance you two thousand dollars as expenses."

"That is very generous of you."

"The box is very important. We could hardly be more determined to get it."

"I see. Your own efforts have failed?"

Mr. Chaing spread his hands deprecatingly. "Mr. Cantey, we are business men. Such things are beyond our poor abilities. I must warn you that unscrupulous people are now in possession of this box. They would think nothing of cutting your throat."

"So I imagined. And you and Mr. Kung are patriots." Rayne looked skeptical.

"That, Mr. Cantey, can be checked with our embassy in Washington," said Mr. Chaing rather stiffly.

Rayne nodded. "Of course. However, I do not need to check with Washington, Mr. Chaing. Mr. Kung might be no relation to the Kung who recently figured in certain soy bean speculations—"

Mr. Kung's hissing intake of air indicated that he was.

"—and you may be no relation to the Chaing who figures—just how is somewhat obscure—in a body of men which we shall classify as the China Lobby. When patriots ride in Rolls Royces costing upwards of fifteen thousand dollars and send the stock market into a frenzy at the flick of a finger, one wonders about your prostrate country."

There was a general celestial stiffening and a small silence lasted for a while.

"There have been people," continued Rayne, "who have been unkind enough to suggest that much of the gold advanced China in moments of crisis now reposes in the bank accounts of certain 'patriots.' How do you feel about that, Mr. Chaing?"

Mr. Chaing's face ducked beneath a mask of inscrutability, but Mr. Kung's jaw was slack.

"I shall not dignify calumny with defense, Mr. Cantey. It is possible that we have come to the wrong man."

"It is not only possible, it is probable." Rayne stood up. "I bid you gentlemen good night."

Mr. Chaing stood up and made motion to Mr. Kung, but that worthy did not move. Instead he shot a swift string of Cantonese at Mr. Chaing which Rayne easily understood.

"This has been very badly handled and it shall be reported to other and higher places. You have deliberately antagonized the fool and aroused his ire. We do not care about his suspicions. We need him."

Mr. Chaing sat down abruptly. "Mr. Cantey, let us not become angry. We have great need for your services and if the stipend is not enough, we may bargain."

Rayne smiled to himself and sat down. He was interested and had almost lost a commission. There would have to be a reason for his attitude so he provided one. "I will want half of the money now."

Mr. Chaing demurred. "We are being very generous with your expense money. Why would you risk carrying such a sum with you?"

Rayne put on his most contemptuous look. "The box is worth twenty thousand dollars to you—rather, let us say you are willing to pay that much for it. It must be worth a great deal more. What sort of persuasion do you think I will use on the present owners?"

Mr. Kung chuckled and Mr. Chaing squirmed. "I hadn't thought of that," said the latter.

"Or," added Rayne, "did you expect me to murder him and take it?"

Mr. Chaing produced a convincing shudder. "The very thought offends me."

"Well, what now?"

"May I take it that you have accepted my offer pursuant to your conditions?"

"You may."

Mr. Chaing sighed. "Very well. Will you accept my check for the amount? I do not carry such sums with me."

"The check will be quite satisfactory. Now, suppose you go into the history of this little box somewhat further. I will need something on which to proceed."

Mr. Chaing made a steeple of his hands. "When the Nationalist Government fled China for Formosa, there was necessarily considerable confusion. There became a situation whereby it was difficult to distinguish friend from foe and naturally many valuables were lost, or shall we say stolen. This box was the property of one of the Generalissimo's most trusted aides. I say property, but perhaps I should say responsibility. He, poor man, was murdered but the box was saved by others whose interests were parallel to our own. In the very moment of delivery to the proper persons, they too were shot down in an alley and the box disappeared."

"Where were the last murders committed?"

"In Hong Kong, not very far from the Nationalist consul's abode. It was there that the box was to have been delivered."

"I see. And of course none of the assassins was ever apprehended."

"Of course. Nor, to my knowledge, has the box been seen since. Not by the proper custodians, at least."

Rayne was forced to laugh and he did so with considerable gusto.

"You laugh, Mr. Cantey?"

"I do. Your use of the word 'proper' amused me. Mr. Chaing, I will accept your offer and I hope you will pardon my laughing."

For a second the mask of inscrutability slipped and Rayne knew he was not pardoned.

"There is one thing, Mr. Cantey, that we have not mentioned. Mr. Kung will accompany you."

For a bare instant, Rayne suffered a reaction much like the one produced by the switch cane emulating a pistol shot. In a split second he had hardened, poised on the edge of his chair, his senses thrumming, on guard like an over-stretched wire.

"Well, now," he said, relaxing, his teeth showing in a mirthless grin, "is that a fact? Okay, Charley, if that's the way it has to be, you can ram it. I will not be breathed upon by any 'patriot.' The deal is off and so are you. Get moving."

Kung shot forth another cataract of Cantonese. "You are a fool and I'm sorry I called him one. He obviously is not. Retract that condition immediately."

Chaing spread his hands in a placating gesture. "Naturally, sir, if you do not wish it. There is no reason to become upset. It is of no importance. I merely wished to provide you with protection."

Rayne sniffed contemptuously. "Him..."

Mr. Kung erupted into furious action, his grin very broad, and drew a small Sauer automatic from his left armpit. "I'm very quick—"

There was a thud as the point of Rayne's toe connected with the pistol, another as the gun struck the ceiling and a softer one as he caught it. He handed it back to the stunned Kung.

"So am I. Nevertheless, I shall try to struggle along without you."

Kung took the pistol with nerveless fingers and fumbled it back into place, his face still vacant with surprise.

Mr. Chaing, scarcely able to restrain his delight, and revealing that between the two "patriots" there was little love lost, turned to Rayne. "As I have said, Mr. Cantey, the last we knew of the box it was on the corpse of its bearer in Singing Bird Alley, Hong Kong. I suggest that you begin with our consul there. He will give you all possible aid. Here is a letter to him from me and in another envelope the two thousand dollars in expense money. If you will make a light, I shall be glad to write you a check covering the amount of your stipulations."

CHAPTER TWO

"RAYNE CANTEY!"

Rayne turned to be almost knocked down by an Air Force Major. In the narrow space afforded by the transport, he had little room to maneuver.

"Gatlin," he gasped. "When did you take to the air?"

They pumped hands as Rayne took in the stocky frame with its round face and balding head of sandy hair.

"Boy, it's good to see you," said Gatlin. "Me? Hell, I've been a fly boy, after a fashion, ever since forty-five. Where can you be flying and how did you manage a hitchhike on this important crate?"

Rayne grinned. "That's a long story, but it's one that interested Ed a lot so he fixed it."

"How is Ed, by the way? I haven't seen him since I resigned in forty."

"He's fine, what with bouts with Congress, begging appropriations and what not."

"Yeah, and any story that interests him, interests me. Give."

Rayne gave and the more he talked the deeper grew the crease in Gatlin's forehead. "What sort of fairy story is that?" he scoffed.

"That's what I intend to find out. I was told to deliver the box unopened."

"What's to keep you from opening it and closing it again?"

"Chaing said he'd know if it had been opened and that the ones who had it wouldn't need to open it because they were already wise."

"That much is so. And just what did Ed say to that?"

"He said that if we couldn't open it in his lab and put it back the same way, he'd personally fire Eichelberger."

Gatlin nodded. "If he can't, then no one can. I'll never forget the work he did on that Lumberton kidnapping. That guy is a real wizard. You're on your way to Hong Kong now?"

"That's right."

"Well, how'll you get from Pusan to Hong Kong?"

"There will be a way, I'm sure. Right now I'm thinking of tagging a Limey transport and flying down."

Gatlin nodded. "Sure. I can fix that. I'm not—" He lowered his voice. "I'm not really a fly boy, you know."

"I figured as much. What's happening? The beer being stolen en route?"

"Worse than that, son. I wish I could tell you, but you know how it is—"

"Sure, I know. By the way, you don't know anything about me, either."

"Right, so rather than introduce you to Wingate, I'll write him a note. He's dispatch officer for the Limeys and he'll fix you up."

Wingate was very British and even in Pusan there were such things as moustache wax. He ran his fingers beneath his crisp lip adornment and then cleared his throat.

"Gatlin, eh? Well, well. Haven't had a chance to thank him for that case of scotch. You wouldn't care for a spot, would you?" He looked at Rayne with hopeful discouragement.

Rayne smiled. "No, thanks. I've been living off the fat and I wouldn't want to dip into your grog."

"Now, let's see—you want to pop over to Hong Kong?"

"Right."

"Can't tell me what for, of course."

"Sorry, I can't. It's official—semi-official, I mean."

"Got some identification, I suppose."

Rayne handed him his billfold and Wingate thumbed through the various plastic holders, eyeing each casually. Then he stiffened suddenly and shot Rayne a sharp glance. "So, you're one of those."

"Pardon?"

He tapped a smooth fingernail on the card Rayne had been given at that last interview. "This! I did chores for the Foreign Office once. Met one of your chaps with one of these and it certainly did throw us for a loop. We didn't know what it was, but the boys in the front office did, and they had orders from Downing Street. Roosevelt started the idea, didn't he?"

"I think so."

"Well, naturally you'll be taken care of. Let me see." He dug into a pile of manifests. "Quite! Converted Lancaster leaving at fifteen hundred. In the meantime—a spot of something to wet your whistle. I can offer beer, tea, or ..." he hesitated fractionally, "... or a whiskey and water. Sorry, but soda is a luxury."

"Tea will be fine, if you have time."

"I'll take the time. I don't often see a man of your station. I understand there aren't but a handful."

"Right. Norcross is a friend of mine, by the way."

"Fancy that. The fella has ice water for blood, I think. Never saw such a cool customer. Well, we'll drop over to my digs and see what we can find."

A wizened Chinese houseboy padded ahead of Rayne down a corridor dimly lit by peach-colored bulbs. He knocked on a door that had the dull solidity of plywood. If he had heard any summons it was more than Rayne's ears could pick up, but he opened the door and bowed. Rayne passed through the portal and there the modern garishness of the house ended. The room was dim with costly silk drapes and the furniture had the dull rich lustrous sheen of antiquity, a characteristic of most truly

Chinese furniture, inviting to the eye but revolting to the frame. The desk formed the only modern touch, being of dull mahogany and covered with a modest confusion of papers.

"Mr. Cantey, I believe," said the slender Chinese seated behind the desk. He did not stand but waved a hand toward a carved chair of some yellow wood that Rayne could not identify.

Rayne nodded and took the chair. "News travels fast."

"Our modern world," smiled the man. "I'm Mr. Yang."

"Where is Mr. Yin?"

For a moment the man's muddy eyes clouded, then he laughed. "Ah, yes. I see you are aware of my countryman's poor efforts as a writer."

"Mr. Yutang's efforts are not poor and few men of intelligence are unaware of him."

Rayne did not like the Chinese consul, possibly because he had come prepared to dislike him. His eyes seemed to fit their sockets badly, the skin was stretched too tightly over the small skull, and the hair had largely disappeared. There was a suggestion of a moustache on his upper lip, not unlike a careless smudge of soot.

"The letter I have," said Rayne, taking it from an inside pocket, "is probably superfluous, but I was told to deliver it."

"Ah, yes, of course. I should like to read a letter from the estimable Mr. Chaing." He took the letter, slit it open with a minature *parang* that looked formidable enough for murder. Rayne could see that on the slip of rice paper had been painted vertical lines of characters and some had soaked through slightly, enough that he caught the word "useful" and "interference." His jaw tightened. Not much help. He was certainly considered potentially useful and would not enjoy interference. On the other hand, there might have been some qualifying characters that could easily change the meaning. He had considered steaming the letter open, but he knew from past experience that the character of the paper wouldn't allow it.

Mr. Yang nodded. "A very serious business, Mr. Cantey. I'm yours to command."

"What is a good commodity speculation on the American market at the moment?"

Mr. Yang's carefully expressionless face flickered momentarily, then the smile reappeared. "I'm hardly in a position to answer that."

"No matter. What do you know about a certain box that I'm to recover?"

"I know that there is such a box. I know that it was stolen by brigands who did not stop at murder. Not too far from here, it was. My information is that it is no longer on the Asiatic continent."

"I assumed as much. Had it been I would hardly have been commissioned to find it. Mao thinks little enough of Americans now that his 'volunteers' have had their plow cleaned in Korea."

"It is understandable," said Yang imperturbably. "We have had conflicting reports about the ones who now have it and just where it is." He held up a paper covered with Chinese writing. "This operative says that it is at the moment in the possession of Stanley Moak, a man of many interests and changing fortunes."

Rayne's eyes narrowed. He knew Stanley Moak too well. He was a renegade Englishman who had the soul of a moray and the ethics of a tiger shark. Yang had dubbed him aptly.

"Another operative mentions Mynheer Paul Van der Vanter on Celebes. This I do not quite understand, since Van der Vanter appears from further investigation to be a respectable rubber planter who, until now, has held his plantation under the most adverse circumstances."

"The natives do not love the Dutch."

"And the Boers don't love the British, nor the Filipinos nor the Americans. It is sad."

"Oh, quite sad. What, Mr. Cantey, do you propose to do now? I have told you all I know."

Rayne stood up. "I do not propose to tell you what I will do. You may tell Chaing that I'm on my way."

"You will report, of course?"

"No. When next you hear the chimes of my voice, I shall have the box clutched in my hot little hand. Good day, Mr. Yin—er, Yang." He left amid a heavy silence.

He allowed himself to be wheeled away from the consulate and in the direction of a certain pub of his knowledge, and sank into a speculative reverie. He had come half around the world to find—nothing. Yang's information was little, if any, better than Chaing's. If the operatives thought that Van der Vanter or Stanley Moak had the box, why hadn't they done something about it? In the case of Moak he could understand. Van der Vanter was an honest, if warlike, rubber planter, but Moak would hesitate to kill a man rather less than he would to sip an afternoon gin *pahit*.

"Hey, John," called Rayne, "You savvy him fella place Lick Dawson?"

"Me sabby," said the coolie. "Taking you along there chop-chop."

Rayne sat back. Lick Dawson was a fat Cockney whose fatness was out of character. Rayne had become accustomed to Cockneys as being vinegary little men wearing caps and sharp faces. Dawson looked as little like the picture as Edward Arnold.

A woman staggering beneath the load of an overfat infant was almost run down by the ricksha, earning a heated avalanche of vituperation from the coolie who likened her to a she goat whose hind quarters had been dragging in offal since the days of the seven-headed dragon, whose infant was ill-favored and fated to spend all eternity swabbing the behinds of the lesser gods. Having thus placed himself on record, he scooped up his shafts and took off again. He stopped his ricksha before a blank wall, turned and bowed low.

"You may descend, master, and partake of the wonders of the Dragon of the Yellow Tail and should the women prove ill-favored and smell badly, I, Fang Gat, am acquainted with several whose breasts are as cool and fresh as melons, whose loins are as sweet as musk and whose lips are honey from the comb. Their hair is as the silk from the finest looms and their eagerness and activity is tireless."

"How," asked Rayne, his eyes mere slits of concentration and suspicion, "did you know I spoke Chinese?"

"I was cursing the woman and when I finished, you muttered a word of approval, or so I thought."

"You are very observant. May the gods smile on your house and may your bowels never cry out from emptiness."

"May your progeny be as the sands of the desert," returned Fang Gat, "and may your wives all have small feet and smaller tongues."

"A worthy consideration. But tell me, Fang Gat, am I to pass through this blank wall like a demon?"

"No, master. If you will notice, steps go down and should you follow them, you will find that the Englishman Dawson's place is there and better than I think you have known it before."

"How do you know?"

"Because you looked down the Street of New Dreams when we passed it. It was there that his business once resided—but that was seven years ago."

Rayne's breath hissed as he inhaled slowly. "It seems to me, Fang Gat, that you have eyes in the back of your head and your ears are like the tentacles of a devil fish."

"I was born sharp of ear and poor of pocket. Even now I stand here exchanging pleasantries with you when I might be earning a cash or two."

The white man smiled. "Fang Gat, what do you expect to earn this night, assuming it to be one of your best?"

"Who can say? One night I earned fourteen shillings, but my passengers happened to be fools and drunk in the bargain. You do not appear either drunk or a fool, but my ears seem to detect a proposition. My ears are tentacles again."

"Is Dawson's place exclusively for the amusement of foreign devils?"

"Oh, no. Wealthy Chinese go there. Dawson cares less about the color of a man's skin than he does the color of his money. Master, are you requiring that I enter this establishment for the removal of gravity with you?"

"I am. You have pleased me, Fang Gat."

"I have heard that Americans are great fellows and friendly. I have also heard that they are slightly mad. Now I can believe anything."

"Will you deposit that trap and come with me? I shall be glad to see that you do not lose your fourteen shillings and, moreover, I shall desire transportation back to my hotel when I have seen what fun Dawson has to offer."

Fang Gat seemed to ponder for a moment. "I cannot, as you require, deposit the earner of my bread—there are thieves abroad; nor would Dawson allow me in his place in this attire. If my master will but tender me the fourteen shillings now, I will trot to the miserable collection of sticks where I sleep, gather what few despicable rags I possess, array them as becomingly on my bones as their threadbare condition will allow, and return with my belly filled with stories calculated to cause laughter, and the address of a girl I know whose breasts are as fresh fruit picked from a young tree and whose loins are orchids from the jungles of Sumatra, whose secret is a well of the purest and sweetest oil ..."

Rayne handed him a pound note. "Begone with you and I know I shall not see you again."

"My master's thoughts are his own. I can only say that I shall return even as I have said."

The coolie turned somewhat abruptly, picked up the shafts of his conveyance and disappeared around a bend in the narrow winding street.

The name of the establishment was not discernible as Rayne walked in. Inside the place was all that was British and best with heavy oaken tables and chairs of such poundage that a man wouldn't have been able to swing one with particular facility. The bar was long and of teak, showing dents that might have been caused by thrown bottles had the wood been anything but teak. The mirror was not solid, but broken up into three ovals set at such an angle that there seemed to be six bartenders when there were only two. The interior was large and filled to capacity with chairs and tables, the only open space being a small polished floor which he suspected was for the entertainers.

He touched a desiccated waiter on the arm. "I'd like to see Dawson."

The fellow sized him up until it amounted to an insult. "Not arf you wouldn't."

Rayne's eyes held the other's for a moment. "Maybe you didn't hear me. I said I wanted to see Dawson."

"I 'eard yer the fust time. Dawson's guv orders. No bleedin' crashers in 'is office."

"Oh, so he's in his office. Thanks." Rayne walked on through the smudge of smoke and noise to the back of the building where there was a door presided over by a rather husky fellow with a scar on his chin that made him seem ready to drool at all times.

"Fut vew vant?" asked the man, spittily, who had been watching the byplay between the waiter and Rayne.

"I want to see Dawson."

"Vlow, now! Vawson don't fee novody."

Rayne, whose nerves had been queered by any number of things for the last week, came near to losing his temper. "Is he through that door?"

"Ves. Vhat's vhere 'e ivz. Vhy?"

"None of your business, Spit Lip. Move aside."

"Vlow, I said. Novody goes in vere."

Rayne reached out an arm as stiff as a jib boom, his right foot moving simultaneously. The hand rammed into the fellow's Adam's apple and the foot prevented his feet from retrieving balance. He laughed at the consternation on the upturned face as the man lay at full length on the floor, and walked through the door.

"Well, strike me fer a ruddy Dutchman!" ejaculated the pile of flesh behind the desk. "If you ain't Rayne Cantey, then I'm Mao Tse-tung."

"Do not jest about your potential boss, Lick. How are you?"

Dawson held out a pudgy hand and shook with Rayne. "When 'e gets to be boss, you'll find Dawson pullin' for Singapore or some such place. Tell me, didn't I hear a something of a slight thud outside me door, Cantey?"

"Yes, there was a spitting cobra who disputed my passage."

"You cosh 'im?"

The door opened and the man came in, a shot-loaded bag of leather clutched in his right hand.

"Aht, you blahsted scum," snarled Lick. "I told you a 'unnered times you got to learn a toff by 'is walk and dress. Next time you put yer 'ands on Mr. Cantey 'ere 'e 'as my permission to barsh yer perishin' skull in. Now get aht o' here."

Lick sank back in his chair. "Set down, Mr. Cantey, and tell me what brings you right to the edge o' the flame. I 'ope you'll pardon the 'elp. Ain't a brain in a dozen."

"That's okay, Lick. Tell me—just conversationally speaking, would you like to make twenty thousand cold cash dollars?"

"*Coo,*" Lick blinked rapidly three times. "If you mean genuine Lincoln heads and not Straits dollars, I'd say—'oo wouldn't?"

"Well, I've been offered that to find something for someone."

"Well, you'll find it, I'm thinkin'."

Rayne looked at the fat Englishman closely. "Lick, are you and me still friends?"

Lick sat back and his eyes grew serious. "Them's sorta 'ard words, Mr. Cantey."

"I'm sorry, but this is pretty serious business."

Lick shrugged. "Would I tell you if we wasn't? I got a good memory, Mr. Cantey. I ain't fergot that night in Pandalang—and I'll bet Moak ain't either. He 'ad to change gun 'ands. It was a mistake shootin' 'im in the shoulder. I'd be a skeleton lettin' the breeze through my ribs but for you. If you need somethin', then all you gotta do is tell me. If you need a stake, if you need a quick trip some place where the customs ain't, then Lick Dawson's your man. I'm the same man you drug outa the Glass Canary by the coat tails. I'm the same man what you stuffed full o' cotton wool and kept from bleedin' to death. You name it."

"Thanks, Lick. I just wanted to make sure. The deal is this."

For thirty minutes Rayne talked and Dawson interrupted from time to time to put in a question. Finally Rayne said, "So that's what they want and will pay heavy cash to get."

"The Nationalists want it … hmmm."

"No, I didn't say that. In all fairness I must say that they described themselves as 'patriots.' They said it was vital for the good of China that they recover the box."

Dawson sneered. "Livin' in the lap o' luxury while their 'earts bleed for China. Me, I think more of China than the lot of them." He reached in his desk and brought out a bottle of Metaxa. "Have a sip?"

"Sure." Rayne sat back and relaxed while Dawson filled two tiny glasses with great care, his fat brow beaded with sweat and furrowed deeply in concentration.

"And the ruddy Consul thinks Moak may 'ave it?"

"That's what he said."

"And was there a ricksha waitin' for you just outside like someone had ordered it?"

"That's right. I went there in a taxi, but I didn't know how long I'd have to stay, so I dismissed it. You sound like the thing was prepared—set up."

Dawson nodded. "I'll even name your coolie for you. Fang Gat."

Rayne sat up. "What do you know?"

The fat man handed him the glass and sat back, tasting his own carefully. "I'm a man what knows a good many things, Mr. Cantey. I know 'ow the gold got from the mainland to Formosa. I know 'ow much never arrived and where it is now— any way, the men 'oo 'ad it. Mind you, I never read a stateside paper but I can tell you that the soy bean market went into a steam not long ago."

"That's right. Go ahead."

"Well, this much I can tell you. Yer black box ain't got no gold in it."

"I know that. Too small."

"Right. And this I can tell you, too—there's more than one outfit what wants that box."

Rayne tensed. "You mean there're two outfits that want the box beside the one who has it?"

"That is my meanin'. Two men was killed in Singin' Bird Alley and the box was taken from them. Ten minutes later, the ones what done the killin' was waylaid and two of their number got clobbered but the third got away 'e 'ad the box."

"Would he take it to Celebes and stash it with a Dutch rubber planter?"

"Nah, but he might go there and work on the rubber plantation thinkin', and well, that it 'ud be a good place to 'ole up."

"Aha, that could be it. Tell me, Lick, have you ever come up with a possibility of what might be in that box?"

Dawson shrugged. "I got me doots if the ones what was doin' all the scramblin' and killin' even knew." He shut his huge hand over the tiny glass and inhaled the fragrance for a moment.

"Thing is, what could be in a box that size worth all this money and murder and trouble?"

"I've asked myself that a thousand times and there are some others who would like to know and not from idle curiosity."

Dawson smiled. "You've cut yourself orf from the old job. But once a government man, always a government man, I always say."

"I didn't say a word—"

"I know you didn't." Dawson pulled out a box of expensive cheroots and offered one to Rayne who refused, took one himself and lit it. "There's one thing that might or might not be impor- tant. You say some self-appointed patriot is hirin' you. Well, I might as well tell you that another bunch of 'em, also patriots, is also lookin' for the box."

"Before we get too far away from the subject, what about this Fang Gat? He's a remarkable fellow."

Dawson shot an enigmatic look at Rayne. "That ain't arf. Did you talk to 'im?"

"Yes. I was intrigued and told him I'd pay what he'd likely make if he'd come in with me. I notice you let Chinese in."

Dawson sighed. "Used to keep 'em out, but a shilling's a shil- ling, as I've said before. What'd 'e say?"

"Said he'd go home and dress, but wanted his money first. I'll never see him again."

"Wanta make a light friendly wager?"

"What?"

"If 'e said 'e'd come back, 'e'll be 'ere. You don't attach no sig- nificance to 'im bein' right there under yer nose when you come out of the consulate?"

"Hell, there're rickshas all over the place."

"Not with Fang Gats pullin' 'em. If I was you, I'd cultivate 'im ... 'cept for one thing."

"What's that?"

"It's just possible that you and Gat is on two sides of the fence. When 'e comes, you'll see pretty quick that 'e ain't no garden variety of coolie."

"Then you think he might have been planted at the embassy?"

"I'd bet on it."

Rayne tamped a cigarette on his thumbnail and scowled. "You know what that means, don't you?"

"I'd say it means the other side 'as their peepers on you."

"Exactly, and how did they find out?"

"Don't ever ask me 'ow no Chinaman knows anything. That's one question I can't answer. There may be a leak at the other end, or at this end. 'oo knows where or 'ow. I'd say your people's got the money and these people's got the know and the best men."

Rayne looked up quickly. "What makes you say that?"

Dawson refilled the glasses. "Suppose you wait till you meet Fang Gat and talk with 'im. I'll stay out of the way and you'll see. You can go out back when you leave and come in the front again. I stay 'ealthy and know things because I ain't never seen talkin' with people."

CHAPTER THREE

RAYNE STOOD AT the bar sipping a whiskey and water. The whiskey was far and away better than the water, so much so that it seemed a shame to mix the two. He filed the decision away for future action.

He felt, rather than saw, the well-dressed Chinese come through the door and shoulder up beside him.

"Did I hear you say that you were setting them up?" he asked in cultured English.

Rayne, not a little irritated at the familiarity, said, "If you did then you're fey or something. I neither offered, nor have I any intention of it. Do you have auditory hallucinations?"

"Only rarely. Still, I could have sworn that I heard you offer to buy me a drink."

Rayne, nettled considerably past normal, turned on his stool. "Do I know you?"

"That is as may be. Possibly in some other incarnation ..."

"That's Indian."

"If true, it is universal; if not, it is trash and superstition. I'll take gin and bitter."

"That's the only way you'll get it, if it's left to me."

"Come, come, Mr. Cantey, did you not ask and pay for my company the rest of the evening?"

Rayne started and surveyed the man carefully. "My apologies, Fang Gat. Who would believe that beneath that marvelous suit of Shantung silk reposed a coolie."

Fang Gat grinned personably. "Let us say that beneath the mean garments of the coolie reposed a remarkable Fang Gat."

"I had already assumed that or I wouldn't have asked for your company. Tell the man what you want and I'll pay out Chaing's money as long as it lasts."

His remark startled Fang out of his suave state for the barest fraction of a second.

"Are you," inquired Rayne pointedly, "acquainted with the illustrious Chaing?"

Fang shrugged casually. "It might well be. It is not an unusual name."

"Is it also not unusual that a coolie who makes a dubious living trotting up and down the grades of Hong Kong dragging tourists, makes enough money to possess such elegant rags as you now wear?"

The bartender put out the gin and bitter and Fang lifted the glass. "Cheer ho," he said with perfect intonation.

"Mud in yours too," said Rayne. "To get along…"

"Mr. Cantey, you are as inquisitive as you maintain I am acute."

"I am not without a certain suggestion of acuteness myself."

"Of that I am positive." He faced Rayne and said in a very serious voice, "I think that fundamentally you are a very just man."

"Thanks, no end. And where does that lead?"

Fang shrugged. "I merely made a statement."

"Have you other statements to make?"

"All in good time. This time, allow me to buy."

"On a coolie's wages?"

"I am an artist at fan-tan. The gods have smiled upon me recently."

"I'll have rye and water."

Fang Gat gestured with a slender yellow hand. "Allow me to suggest that we occupy a table. Pulling a public conveyance is not without certain elements of fatigue, especially when it appears that all American tourist women are excessively large."

They sat at a table in a corner away from eyes and, more important, away from ears. Their order was brought by a small, slimly carved daughter of China dressed in scarlet trousers and plum-colored jacket that came below the hips, effectually concealing whatever charms her slightness might have afforded.

"We dress our women better," said Rayne critically as the girl padded from view.

"Ancient and honorable virtues must be maintained."

"Nuts. People are people."

Fang Gat laughed soundlessly. "Illustrious K'ung Fu Tze couldn't have put it better."

Rayne toyed with his drink. "Fang, there have been a series of circumstances today that seem to conform to some mysterious pattern. I wonder if you could enlighten me?"

As Fang shrugged, Rayne noted that there was little padding in the shoulders of his suit other than that provided by the wearer, which was not inconsiderable. "All things are possible— but then I am not the possessor of all knowledge."

"And neither are the next hundred men one meets."

"Specifically what has seemed out of the ordinary?"

"That you were fortuitously in front of the Chinese Consulate when I came down the steps."

"Had I not been, as you say, fortuitously there, then it is axiomatic that I would have been some place else, fortuitously or ..." he shrugged.

"You would have been some place else all right. However, let us leave that for a moment. Since when do coolies dress in hundred dollar suits?"

Fang Gat's grin was as genuine as his teeth were white. "Patience, thrift, and industry," he said.

Rayne's hand gripped his companion's shoulder and found it as solid as a teak bar. "The coolies I know are thin because one doesn't get fat on a diet of fish and rice. I am not entirely a stranger in this part of the world, my friend. Let me go on record as saying this whole thing has a decided odor."

Fang Gat's face lost its look of bland innocence. "Mr. Cantey, you are now working for a certain group of men whose nationality and my own happen to be identical. Is that not true?"

Rayne's angled face broke into a smile. "Now we proceed. You know who I am and you know for whom I work. The pattern is finished."

"It was not my desire to needlessly keep you in the dark, but we are in a very precarious position. I must bargain with you and I must know as much as I can. Please believe me when I say I wish you no harm personally. But I will tell you now that if it is within my power, you will never deliver that box to Chaing."

Rayne gazed through his glass at a dim light, sipped his drink, then lit a cigarette. All the while his mind was racing furiously. "Then your best bet is to stop me."

"On the contrary. To do that would necessitate killing you. I am not a member of a band of murderers. Perhaps I had better explain a few things."

"Maybe you'd better," agreed Rayne, sitting back. There was a silence during which Rayne saw the keen eyes of Fang sweep the tables before them, then settle back on him.

"I hold a Ph.D. from the University of Southern California. I know Americans and like them. I know that in this sealed metal box there is something highly valuable to a certain group whose love for China has not been convincingly demonstrated. The exact nature of its contents are known to very few. There has been all sorts of speculation regarding this box, but speculation, however good, must fall before facts. Frankly, we do not know. We have operated on the theory that if they are so frantically determined to recover it, then we are just as determined that they do not. Whatever is good for this group will not be good for China. This much is certain. The good of China I would not have in their hands, as those hands are already red with the blood and misery of too many innocent people."

Rayne played with his drink. Suddenly he emptied it and, catching the girl's eye, motioned to her. "Little Peony, would you honor this member of a barbarian race with the sweet sweat of your brow to the extent of refilling our wretched glasses?" He said this in flawless Cantonese and she dimpled prettily.

"That such an honor should be visited upon me, a mere woman, twice in one night is more than my soul can be readily expected to endure. I go, but I shall return."

"Now you know something?" said Rayne grinning. "That chick can take it and hand it back."

"The world moves swiftly in these times. In the day of my father, she should have giggled prettily and disappeared. For the temerity of her recent speech, she would have been beaten with rattan."

"Devil take your ancient customs. So your group is dedicated to effecting my failure. Is that it?"

Fang Gat squirmed uncomfortably. "That is not the way I would put it. Let us say that we desire that you understand our goal and sympathize with it."

"How much is my sympathy worth?"

The face across the table hardened. "How much did Chaing offer?"

"Twenty thousand and expenses."

Fang Gat's face hardened even more. "Mr. Cantey, I give you my word of honor, as one gentleman to another, that the entire resources of my group does not run to half that."

Rayne's eyes traveled unconsciously to the expensive suit, the clothes replacing Chaing's Rolls Royce in his mind for a moment.

"If you are thinking about my clothes, please do not allow them to disturb you. My father is a merchant in this city. For what you would have to pay for it, he can make three new ones."

Rayne nodded and accepted his drink from the lacquered tray and tipped the girl heavily, who then smiled and withdrew. As she moved away, a man dressed in a rusty but still serviceable tuxedo approached the table and placed a folded note in Rayne's palm.

"Pardon me for a moment."

Fang Gat inclined his head in polite permission and lit a long brown cigarette. He sipped his drink and glanced aimlessly about the place.

The note was in a hasty, but legible scrawl. "The woman waiting on your table was hired tonight." That was all. He crumpled the note and thrust it into the pocket of his jacket. He recognized Lick's fist and another quantity had inserted a finger into the pattern.

Rayne lifted his amber eyes to rest on the sloe black ones of Fang Gat. "My friend, tomorrow I intend to leave this city. Where am I going and by what means shall I travel?"

"You will probably travel by boat that will certainly be manned by Chinese or Malays, maybe Kanakas. You will not travel alone, Mr. Cantey."

Rayne nodded at the thrown gauntlet. "I see. I shall be watched, but you'd prefer that I give you some assurance of my sympathy."

"I had hoped we might reach some agreement."

Rayne laughed. "Fang, old fellow, don't you realize that you are not bargaining? You are delivering an ultimatum."

Fang's face grew pained. "Please believe me, sir, such is not our attitude. Nevertheless, it must be admitted that we have slight latitude. What you will do will be, we are certain, of inestimable value to the worst enemies of our country. Did you never wonder what became of the millions of dollars your country has poured

33

into China? Did you never wonder why it was that the Nationalist Army went to pieces like stale bread in a downpour? Another thing, has there been no excitement over the enormous amount of American equipment used in Korea by the Communists? Where did it come from?"

"Some say it came from Russia."

Fang Gat leaned forward, his face tight with intensity. "Mr. Cantey, do you not know—indeed, does not all America know—that the material delivered to Russia by you during the last war was so vastly superior to anything they could produce that they, at this very moment, wouldn't part with a monkey wrench of it? It is true that they have some good weapons, they have good tanks and, of late, they have produced some excellent fighter planes. But..." He sat back and mopped sweat from his brow. "I can only ask that you take my word for it. My position in the Nationalist Army was Colonel of the 'Eyes of the Night' Regiment. I know whereof I speak. At this moment I would be on Formosa with my men, were it not for other and more important things for an educated man to do. Mr. Cantey, I beg of you—do not carry out this mission. I implore you, do not deal tottering China this last blow."

Rayne was strangely moved by the man's almost phrenetic eagerness and obvious sincerity. He bit his lip for a moment, and then he said, "What do you want me to do?"

"Help us find it. Be with us when we open it, see for yourself what is in it." He relaxed and spread his hands on the table. "And we would then be most grateful for any advice you might give. We have found that the mass of the American people are among the very best friends China has. Your people are generous to a fault, they abhor cruelty and suffering. It is not right that the money that they have so cheerfully given should find its way into the pockets of a few bloated, heartless materialists who will exploit my country until the last peasant is starved into a skinful of pitiful bones. Mr. Cantey, have you ever been in China?"

"Yes," Rayne's voice sounded slightly disembodied.

"Then you know whereof I speak." Fang spread his hands in a helpless gesture. "If we fail to sway you, then we will be forced to use other measures. This you must not take as a threat, but as an honest projection of our plans."

Rayne ordered again and when the drinks came, he tasted it carefully, but it seemed to be honest rye and Hong Kong water. "Fang, what do you know of me?"

"We know your name. We know of your record in the war. We know of your job and that you recently resigned."

"Did you know that I saw my old boss before coming over here?"

Fang Gat sat upright with a snap. "We did not know that. Then—"

"No, nothing like that, but you may rest assured that I am keeping an eye open for the good of my own country—unofficially. That is one thing Chaing does not know. I am a man of some means. His paltry twenty thousand dollars is waste paper—at least, where something like this is concerned. Does that satisfy you?"

The yellow man licked his lips nervously. "Then you do not intend that the box shall go to Chaing unopened?"

"He said he'd know if it were opened."

"He's very probably a liar. In any event, we have craftsmen here who can open it and no one will be the wiser. Mr. Cantey, let me say this one thing more. It is my most profound belief that whatever, in this particular case, is for the best interests of your country is also for the best interests of mine."

Rayne tapped a cigarette on his thumbnail, lit it and sat back smiling. "Fang Gat, two hours ago I did not know you lived and now I am asked to accept you. And not only you, but a shadowy 'group,' at your stated value. I do not wish to be unkind, but did you really think that I'd fall for this just because you happen to be a handsome, well spoken man, once of Southern Cal, and toss twenty thousand smackers in the fire?"

Fang Gat's face dropped and a look of hopelessness covered it. From his murky black eyes there shot forth little flecks of metallic light which Rayne did not miss. "I'm sorry, Mr. Cantey. I was certain for a moment that you would be with us. I'm bitterly sorry."

"Wait, man—can't you see my side of this? Can't you give me any proof that you are in reality Fang Gat, a Colonel in the Nationalist Army and a patriot? You say you are, how do I know? You certainly didn't depend on anything I might say for your knowledge of me."

"I see. Yes, I suppose there's something in what you say. Mr. Cantey, will you accompany me to my father's house?"

"I can do no less than that. I asked for proof and I suppose you're ready to produce it."

"Unfortunately, I'm afraid that what proof I have for you is not what you would call conclusive. Just the same, I will make an attempt. Allow me to take care of the bill."

On the street they looked about for a moment, then hailed a taxi. As they got in, Rayne turned to Fang.

"Did you know that the woman who waited on us had only just been hired?"

Fang nodded easily. "Oh, quite! She's my youngest sister."

Rayne swallowed and grasped the arm cord as the taxi careened around a sharp corner. Through long habit, he glanced behind, but could detect nothing to indicate that they were being followed.

"What was the idea of stashing your sister in that spot?"

"We knew of your friendship with Dawson. Actually, she and others were there for your protection."

"You mean the third group might not like for me to be digging around?"

"You are approximately right. It would also look bad should we be seen together. I don't think Chaing knows my face, but he knows of me and you may be certain that there are others here whose interest in you is not of the least. Did you know that we were followed from the Consulate?"

"No. Who?"

Fang shrugged. "From the Consulate itself. I have a rear view mirror on the shaft of my conveyance. It once inhabited a jeep but I find it useful. That disturbance I raised when the woman crossed our path was of a purpose. They were too close and had to turn into an alley to prevent discovery. We lost them then."

"You hope. If I were any—Look out!"

The taxi swerved away from a car charging out of a sidestreet, climbed the low gutter and smashed head-on into the wall of a teahouse which began to disgorge frightened patrons screeching at the tops of their voices.

"Get out on the street side. Have you a gun?"

"Yes," said Rayne, scuttling out of a providentially open door to the sidewalk. He straightened up cautiously and a bullet spanged off the top of the cab, while another smashed a window six inches from Rayne's head. The driver, who had been shaking his fists at the car and delivering a tirade in Chinese, ducked prudently out of sight.

Rayne suddenly became as cool as morning. He lent a quick hand to Fang and as the car backed up to get a clearer shot at them, he rested his hand on the back of the cab and shot the driver through the head. Patrons now screamed their way back into the tea shop in an irresistible tide, cracking doorfacings and caving in plate glass.

Fang drew an ancient but serviceable Mauser, and thundered away at the car whose occupants, now bereft of their driver, were screeching at each other and trying to abandon ship. One more shot they managed to get away with; it effectively sprayed Rayne's face with fine glass, but the marksman died knowing that he had missed. Rayne's .45 bellowed like a field gun in the narrow confines of the street and the man fell against those ahead of him as they all tried to get out of the door at once. One man made it alive and sprinted down the street, his heels flying up high as he strove mightily to escape. Fang laughed softly, and threw the long barrel of his weapon across the crook of his elbow and loosed a single shot. The fleeing man skidded sickeningly into a doorway, bursting it open and causing a fresh chorus of wails to fill the air as the occupants lodged within gave tongue to their protests.

Police whistles began to bleat nearby and a very official looking Daimler nosed down the street with the driver cursing the mob that had gathered. Constables were on either front fender, alternately blatting with their whistles and coshing members of the crowd that got too close to the car.

"To quote a Chinese-American proverb," said Fang calmly, "there is a time for fishing and a time for drying nets. Let us disappear through this alley here that seems made for such escapes."

The alley stank higher than heaven and seemed populated by all manner of obstacles, not the least of which were snarling animals Rayne took for dogs. Doubting that they had been inoculated against rabies, he lashed out with his feet every time he heard a growl, once almost breaking a toe against a brick. They threaded their way through the narrow escapeway until they came to another street and hailed a cruising taxi.

The home of Fang Gat's father was not outwardly impressive, being a mere door over which were splashed several Chinese characters. Fang managed entry in a manner that escaped Rayne and he was led into the dim corridor that had a smell of ages of incense and other odors that were not easily identified.

"If you will wait here a moment, I'll prepare the family for your company." Fang disappeared and Rayne found himself in a very plain room with low silk upholstered couches. Its very simplicity and atmosphere seemed to identify it as a room that visitors used to await audience with the family in another part of the house.

Fang came back, now dressed in black silk trousers and a quilted mandarin coat. "This is a concession to my father. He likes to keep his house a part of China. He'll take the foreign devil's money gladly, but he will have none of his ways. His children's habits provide some of his bitterest complaints. We may see him now."

There were other dim corridors that finally led to a massive carved teak door which was opened by Fang.

"My father," said Fang, as he ushered Rayne in, "I have the honor to present in this house, Rayne Cantey from America."

"Come closer, my son, as my eyes are bad," said the old man kindly. "It is said that you speak our language."

"It is one of my prized talents," said Rayne in Cantonese, bowing low. "Please accept my apologies for this visit."

"My son has explained. You are welcome to the house of Fang. Please be seated."

The article was hardly a chair, and yet not a couch, but it was heavy and richly carved and the cushion was soft. The room was large with walls lacquered in canary yellow and hung with pale blue draperies, hand painted with line drawings of peaceful garden scenes, women serving tea, and children sitting respectfully by with their hands placidly held in their laps. Fang So was wrinkled and spare as a sandpiper, sitting like a starved Buddha on his crossed legs, his scanty moustache drooping almost to his chin.

"This man," began Fang Gat, "is in the employ of certain men of whom we know, headed by one Chaing. He is not unkindly disposed toward us and wishes some assurance that the cause we represent has none of the grasping craven intents such as we know inhabit his employers."

For a moment Fang So sat immobile and Rayne had the impression that he would like to spit. Then he looked at his son, his beady eyes flashing. "It is to be hoped that Chaing's reward will be to be buried in a dung heap with no one to mourn at his grave and that his soul will grill until the end of time on the coals of his treachery. He and all like him." He turned to Rayne. "I ask you your pardon for this unseemly outburst, but the very name of the man fills my belly with bitter foam. It is because of him and others of his breed that China now is prostrate and overlorded by fools of our own race. What, Mr. Cantey, can we do to prove that we are not as the despicable Chaing?"

"It grieves me that I am put in this position," said Rayne, heartily wishing that there was some way out of his position. "That I should be suspicious of your motives is an ache to my bowels, but—"

The old man held up a clawlike hand. "An honest man does not wear virtue around his neck, nor may a man look into the eyes of a criminal and see a record of his crimes. It is unfortunate but true that a fool and a wise man may look alike. You are a cautious man because your profession is an exacting one. No apology is necessary."

"Then the burden of proof, I regret to say, lies on your side."

"Being an American, you speak to the point. Is it possible that you know this Chaing well?"

"Well enough. We've had our eyes on him for some time."

"Then by inference, may it not be that since we are against him, we are not as you suspect?"

Rayne smiled. "When I am your age I should gloat over one-tenth of your wit. By inference, I can arrive at part of what I want. Let us say, for the moment, that you have slaughtered my suspicions. What happens then?"

The old man looked at him for an uncomfortable space, then spoke. "My son was educated among men such as you, and his report is gratifying where it touches on you personally. It is indeed fortunate that there is no suspicion of you in this house. We believe you to be a man of integrity and courage. We have reasons for so believing. We know of your work during the war— that you were a soldier and a man of the shadows at the same time, that you gave to your country two men in the form of one.

Had we not known all this, it is possible that our methods might have been different."

Rayne nodded soberly. "I have pondered on that. It would be simple to kill me and ..."

"But in that sort of simplicity is folly. Mr. Cantey, we find that we not only want your help in recovering this box, but we shall be highly honored if you will advise us when we view its contents. We are business men largely and, in a manner of speaking, intrigue is foreign to us. We are not diplomats, nor are we men whose minds span international vistas. We need your muscle, but even more, we need your mind. Gat tells me that you have mentioned money. I am what might be called a prosperous merchant, but much of my prosperity goes for food and medicines for my people, as does the prosperity of many others of us. I will, however, make you this pledge. If you will help us, I promise you that you will be paid the twenty thousand dollars. Possibly it will take some time and I have no doubt that on the shoulders of my son will fall the greater part of the burden. I am an old man and any morning might see my spirit on its way to the gods. I can give you nothing in the way of proof of my intentions. I can only give you my word and remember the day when a man's word was all that was necessary."

Rayne stood up, his face flushed and angry. Angry at himself, angry at the strangling lump that had come to his throat. "I am in the dust at your venerable feet. A man can become suspicious by habit and habit often becomes a disease. Many things have happened recently and my mind is crowded to the bursting. I beg forgiveness for the things I did not see before. In what way may I serve you?"

Fang So spread his hands slowly. "It is very simple. Allow my son to accompany you."

Rayne sat down heavily. "That is simple enough, it is true. It happens at the moment that I have little direction myself."

"It has been said that a man by the name of Moak, an Englishman, has the much-coveted box. Others say it is held by a rubber planter on Celebes."

"I was told that also, and unless our sources are common ones, I find it odd that they should both say the same thing."

Fang Gat sat up straight. "May I ask if that information came through the Consulate?"

"It did."

The other's eyes narrowed calculatingly. "Now, that becomes interesting. We paid for our information, and it would appear that others paid for it too. A merchant of some industry, one might say." Fang Gat frowned.

"Why," asked Fang So, "would an honest, hard-driving planter of rubber foul his hands with such a thing? And how was it accomplished?"

"That is a question I have pondered upon. It has been suggested that possibly the person holding the box is not really Van der Vanter, but someone in his employ."

"A plausible suggestion," put in Fang Gat. "One that appeals to me. But how then did the news leak out?"

Rayne shrugged. "Of what use is the box if he has to stay in hiding? He probably tried to get the information back to certain people and put a price on it. The bearer of the information put it to his own advantage. It is entirely possible that I am the one the information was supposed to reach. But I doubt that it was intended to reach you."

"In a thing like this," said the old man, "it is a matter of trial and error, of search and possible discovery. Can we then depend on your assistance, Mr. Cantey?"

Rayne breathed deeply. The answer rested on his next words. "Fang So, I can say this only. I will let Fang Gat go with me. We will be brothers in this search. When the box is found it will be opened and I shall act in the best interests of my government regarding the contents. Money or other valuables we do not care about. I doubt that such is among the contents because of the small size of the container. Fang Gat has suggested the possibility that our interests might be the same. It is to be hoped that they are. That is all I can promise."

"Well spoken, my son. We cannot expect the world for the asking. The money…."

"There will be no more talk of money," barked Rayne, acutely conscious of his red face. "When I mentioned it to Fang Gat, I was merely feeling my way. Your family will not be burdened with any such debt. I am a man whose father was provident and wise. His worldly goods leave me with more than is my due."

Fang So's eyes softened. "A man's due is not to be reckoned in terms of gold. Your modesty is becoming, but remember that we know of your worth to your country. The lack of men like you is why we are blundering about in circles trying to recover something from the fire that is China, that she may once again look toward the sun, that her starving millions may be fed; that the lot of a child born within her unhappy boundaries may be something other than to hunger and shiver and should he live, perchance, through such rigors, shoulder a rifle and do battle against his brothers."

" 'e's a perishin' mongrel," Lick Dawson was saying, "but 'oo ain't in these latitudes? Meanin' no disrespect to the many Chinese who are mostly pure." He inclined his head to Fang Gat. "Thing is, 'e goes straight to where you want to go or near enough. Got any idea where this cheese eater's rubber grove is?"

Fang Gat nodded. "It is supposed to be somewhere between Monado and Gorontalo."

"That 'somewhere' is sorta vague and that ain't the way it was told to me."

Rayne blinked. "You too?"

Lick nodded and grinned. "I didn't pay as much as some others. Man says to me that Van der Vanter 'as 'oldin's all over, but what with war and this and that, 'e operates only the biggest now and that's thirty miles or so back country from Mojene."

"One moment," said Rayne as he lifted the telephone. "I'll see if there are any more places that this bird dreamed up." He held the phone for a long time before he heard the sleepy voice of Yang.

"Yang, this is Rayne Cantey. I failed to ask where on Celebes Van der Vanter's plantation is located. It's a fairly large island, you know."

He listened, then muttered a careless thanks and hung up. "Well, we have our work cut out for us. Yang's information said between Macassar and Potopo."

Lick laughed and produced a small map of the Indies. " 'e covered it pretty well, I'd say."

Fang Gat chuckled softly. "And he wasn't as big a fool or liar as he may seem."

" 'ow's that?"

Rayne also looked up from the map, interested.

Fang Gat lifted his shoulders infinitesimally. "The more we blunder about asking, the sooner the word will be passed along and when, after trials and fever, we arrive more dead than alive, as the travelogues put it, he, she, or they will be well prepared."

"I also think the word was supposed to get to others too."

"Yes, and you can bank on it," said Lick. " 'e 'ad no way to contack 'is man direck, so 'e put out the word broadcast sort of, 'opin' the right man'd get it."

"Yes, and he wasn't worried about who else might come nosing around either. The more I know, the less I like it."

"Just wait," predicted Lick. "Ever been in the jungle?"

"Plenty," said Rayne, his lips tight. "Depending on what jungle, they're not too bad."

"The one you're goin' in is bad," said Lick, shaking his head. "Now, about transportation. This mongrel 'as a schooner of sorts and 'e knows the waters from Timor to Hokkaido. Some as says 'e was a pirate once, but since the war operatin' out o' Macao is so good that 'e don't 'ave to pirate no more. You've heard about Macao?"

Rayne nodded. "I rather suspect it is a repository for some gold that was supposed to go to China."

"Well ..." Lick looked at a large watch strapped to his wrist, " 'e leaves tomorrow. What time can you pull your 'ook?"

"I can be ready in an hour."

" 'ere or at the South Basin quay?"

"Either place."

"I'll run you over in my motor boat. Just a jump across the straits. Thirty miles or so."

CHAPTER FOUR

THE SUN HAD fallen on them an hour ago like the flat of an immense gong and the world was a sunstruck sea. The *Lena,* a schooner of some hundred and twenty tons, nosed along like a porpoise with nothing to do, knocking up clouds of spray from the improbably blue water and sending flying fish skittering before her blunt bows to skip from wave to wave until they lost their momentum and dunked clumsily back into the brine.

Fang Gat and Rayne sat in the shade of the deck house and sweated with that abandon seen only in climes where the humidity is at saturation point.

The captain, a heavy man, with the rolling gait of a seasoned seafarer, strolled past without giving them a glance. He was thick of chest and belly and his arms were ape long. At the moment, it seemed that his Occidental blood had all but overpowered his Malay, Melanesian and Polynesian mixture because he had run heavily to flesh and was covered from the waist up, at least, with a notable pelt of reddish shag. One ear had met with accident and was gone, with only a ragged porthole to show where it had been.

"What impression does the captain make upon your sensibilities?"

Fang Gat shrugged resignedly. "Aside from offending them in many ways, you mean? Did you hear what that great stevedore said of him as we were shoving off?"

"No."

"He said that his mother had been a diseased whore on the beach at Banderjasmin whereupon she met and coupled with a pig of uncertain but noticeably inferior lineage. As far as can be seen, that is about as good a remark as I could dream up."

"I don't know. What you told that woman yesterday was something. I'll have to remember that."

"Ahhh," hissed Fang Gat. "I was not aware that there were passengers other than ourselves and the tall one-eyed Chinese."

"Are there?"

"Look forward. What a figurehead she'd make."

Rayne looked and for the first time in years, his stomach did a half roll and stopped sideways, half strangling him.

Her hair was as black as ink and cut square at her shoulders; in the wind it appeared so fine that it bothered her being as it was at the mercy of every gust. On her forehead it was worn in a pointed bang that lent her face a heart-shaped poignance which her full, rather sensitive lips heightened and her somber dark eyes solidified. Her waist was small but her hips swelled in symmetrical sufficiency as did her breasts—high, firm and pointed, showing that in her ancestry there was native blood.

"By the horns of Buddha..."

"Please," murmured Fang Gat humorously. "No blasphemy. Buddha had no horns."

Rayne made a face, then composed his features—she had turned her back to the sea and was watching them. She held their eyes for a moment with the sober steadiness of a child, then turned away and disappeared.

"You of the many eyes," breathed Rayne as he relaxed his taut muscles. "Who is she?"

"I do not know. I but just saw her."

"What is she?"

"I'd say she is the daughter of some rich merchant or planter going home from the convent at Macao. Except I didn't know they let them wear anything at the convent but horrid shapeless habits. Her clothes were quite chic, but definitely Islandish."

"How do you mean?"

"Well, the blouse, for instance. Obviously she wears nothing under it—it is thin and rather off the shoulders, and the swell of her breasts was clearly visible. Her skirt is made of what we call ... when I say 'we', I mean in America ... island print, cut full for coolness and doubtless nothing under that either. Her limbs were not hard to outline beneath it."

Rayne mopped his head, face and neck, feeling that some of the sweat had little relationship to the heat. "I wonder if anyone is with her?"

"There is one who might be. He wears the garb of a cleric. I said the tall Chinese was the only other passenger, but I had forgotten this cleric."

Away to starboard, the smoky bulk of Hainan came into view and as the day waxed older and hotter, it gradually disappeared.

After a dinner that was surprisingly good, consisting of curried chicken and rice, avocado salad with an excellent dressing and—most welcome of all—ice box ice cream, Rayne and Fang Gat sought the deck again, hoping to let the cooler breeze carry off the day's accumulation of heat.

"Are you married, my friend?" asked Fang as they smoked thin cheroots, tapping the ash to windward.

Rayne laughed. "You're the damndest Chinese I ever saw. I thought that wasn't considered a polite question."

"I was in the States for several years, remember?" said Fang smiling.

"No, I'm not married. Are you?"

Fang Gat frowned. "No, and I am an example of what happens when a man steps out of his element. In the years I was at Southern Cal, I dated many women. Some of them were Chinese, but in common with many of us, I was partial to blondes. Being Chinese I didn't have the freest access into the best homes, so I took what I could get in the way of blondes. However, being on the football and basketball teams was something of a help socially and I fell in love with a girl from San Bernadino. She honored me with her affections until the weekend I went home with her. Her parents were polite." Fang Gat stopped and looked back at the turmoil of phosphorescence in their wake.

Rayne nodded. "Her parents were polite. I don't think that could have been put much better. What happened?"

"She was withdrawn from school and sent to a seminary in Chicago. I heard later that she was very unhappy and joined the Red Cross during the war. After that there was a hiatus still existing. I have no idea what became of her."

Rayne flicked a length of ash from his cheroot and watched it shatter against the rail as the wind took it. "I've been too busy for women, except in my lighter moments which have been too few."

"Of women there has been more than enough in my life," said Fang Gat. "My sisters, all moderns, are eternally bringing their friends to the house or arranging a party so that we can meet. It has been rather productive, speaking in terms of joy."

Rayne sighed. "I could use some joy. I wonder where our delightful fellow passenger is?"

"Her dinner was served in her cabin where she ate with her guardian. So much I learned from the steward."

"I wonder who he is?"

"A professional traveling companion provided by the convent, no doubt."

"It appears that they chose the meanest of conveyances."

"Maybe they were in a hurry, too."

Rayne shook his head. "I don't like it. I can feel these things."

"I hope you are wrong."

"So do I. I have other things to think about. What did you find out about the tall Chinese?"

Fang Gat inhaled blue smoke and blew it toward the blob of color the moon was making in its effort to rise. "Nothing good. He came aboard after we did and paid double fare for the privilege of sleeping on deck. There are only two cabins besides the captain's and the crew's quarters below deck."

"If they can sleep there, I'll always wonder how. I'm also wondering how we are going to sleep in that piano box we've been stuck into."

It was one of those quirks of accoustics or a flaw in the wind, but the words were borne to their ears in a clear burst... "good money, but women like her come high..."

Rayne bucked to the jerk of his muscles and two knots appeared on each side of his jaws. Without a word, he glided away from the rail and sidled along the deck house until he could peer through a porthole into the captain's cabin. The hole was obscured by dirty draw curtains, but he listened intently.

"Tellin' you, Perez, that low fare fer two people wasn't no accident."

"But look, my friend. I am a man in a highly respected position. For such a deed I shall have to go far and fast. The police of three continents will be on my trail."

"A thousand pounds is a lot of money."

"Ten thousand is not too much. Remember, Granger—there isn't one like her in the East. She's a pearl, completely untouched as yet. A virgin, all filled with the accumulated passions stimulated by the convent and the things girls will talk and think about in such a place. She wouldn't agree to me staying in her cabin, curtain or no curtain, so I had to bunk with you—she's that particular."

Granger sucked noisily on a black pipe and seemed to consider. "A thousand pounds is more'n I'll make on this whole voyage."

"What is one trip? You'll make many more and with those you've already made..."

"Done. Pay you in the mornin'. Now where's her key?"

"No, no, my friend. I couldn't let you do that. After I get the thousand, you'll get the key. I would prefer the money in sovereigns."

"Where the hell would I get a sovereign?"

Rayne could almost feel Perez's smile. "I rather think you keep quite a store of them aboard, Granger. Not minted in England, of course, but in France, but they are English gold pieces and with the right amount of gold in them."

"My friend," said the captain in a hoarse rumble, "you know too much."

"Only a thousand pounds. That's all I know. And for nothing, I'll give you some advice."

"What's that?"

"Don't try to carry her with you. Put her away on an island—there must be several you know of—and pay some chief for her keep and protection. In that way you won't be running any risk."

Granger erupted in a bellow of laughter. "Son, I got to hand it to you. You really got a head on your shoulders. I got just the place. But I'm not too sure about those passengers Lick Dawson brought me. That American don't look too hot to me and that Chinaman—looks like I seen 'im some place and the recollection ain't a good one."

A gust of fetid air came from the cabin and Rayne's nostrils wrinkled against the stench. Sweat crawled down his back at the thought of what lay in store for the girl. He had a flash of a picture of her writhing in Granger's grasp, her fine long legs being bared by a thick, dirty hand, of putrid lips slobbering over her fine soft mouth.

"But," continued Granger, "I got a place for them, too. They want to go to Celebes. Well, this place will be near enough."

Rayne reeled away from the porthole and mopped his drenched face as he approached Fang Gat. "Things," he breathed, striving to control his voice, "begin to happen."

"Ahhh," Fang Gat's exhalation spoke more than words. "You heard, I take it."

"I heard plenty. Listen to a short version—"

"How long you two been here?" bellowed a voice. Turning, they saw Granger bearing down on them, his face red and furious.

"I can't see that it's any of your damned business," retorted Rayne, leaning away from the rail, balanced like a cat, his arms hanging freely by his sides.

Granger, seeing the move, halted and rubbed his whiskered chin. "I thought you was at dinner."

"Am I responsible for what you thought?"

The captain glowered at them for a moment, then, as an idea struck him, he grinned evilly, showing blackened stubs of teeth. He nodded. "Just askin'. No need for excitement ... gentlemen." He turned on his heel and walked rapidly aft.

"A very transparent man," said Fang Gat, letting his Mauser fall back in its holster beneath his left arm.

"In what way?"

"He was balked there for a moment but the windows of his mind opened and I could see the thought born. What if they did hear? What can they do?' "

Rayne shook his shoulders to rid them of their tense ache. "They could beat his gross head into a pulp and throw him over the side. In fact, I had just such a wild idea for a moment."

"You mentioned a short version a moment ago ..."

"Oh, yes." Rayne related a précis of the conversation.

Fang Gat straightened up. "So. It would appear that we will stop before we are well begun."

"Why?"

"I cannot see him taking us within easy distance of Celebes and putting us off. If he puts us ashore on any number of ten thousand possible islands, it will be one that will come over the horizon soon or I have calculated wrong."

The next morning, there was a long conference between Granger and Perez; when they had finished, the sun was beaming down with such brutal force that Fang Gat was suffering as much as Rayne and had not changed to a pair of shorts as had the latter.

"One of us had better remain armed," he explained quietly.

"I'm glad you elected yourself. This is about as much as a man can endure."

The girl came around the corner of the deck then and both men leaped to their feet.

She smiled and Rayne almost choked on the pressure in his throat. "Please remain seated. It is much too hot for social gestures."

"Little flower," said Fang Gat gallantly, seeing that Rayne could say nothing at all, "your eyes, like peonies in a fabulous garden, see all and understand everything. Think not, however, that mere mortals such as we could remain seated in the presence of divinity."

Her laughter was musical and soft and Rayne struggled frantically for something to say, but again it was Fang Gat who stepped into the breach.

"Since we are fellow passengers might we be honored with your name?"

"Of course. How stupid of me. I'm Taneeta Barstowe."

"May I present Mr. Rayne Cantey of the United States, while I am first in line of the lowly house of Fang, Gat of the given name."

She nodded politely. "Where are you going?"

Fang spoke quickly. "We are on our way to Surabaya."

"But I understood we were going no further than Sandakan."

"Is that your home?"

"Yes. My father and mother keep the mission there."

Rayne found his voice. "That sounds Protestant. You have been to a convent, haven't you?"

"Oh, yes—in Macao. Brother Peter Perez was coming and since it would save money, Mother Mary suggested that I come with him. My father doesn't care for convents, but he made me go anyway."

"This Brother Perez—do you like him?"

"Oh, certainly. Why he's…" Her face underwent a swift change. "No. I retract that. I do not like him."

"Why?" asked Rayne curiously.

"Because he's—I don't know how to say it. He's—he wanted to stay in the cabin with me and put up some sort of curtain. I wouldn't have it. I don't like the way he looks at me and somehow I—" She shook her head. "I must be wrong."

"Tell us," said Fang Gat in a voice so deceptively gentle that Rayne looked at him guiltily.

"I've wondered if he really is a Brother," she blurted uncertainly.

"You didn't know him before this trip?"

"No, I had never seen him before but Mother said he was…" Her head went up. "I don't really remember what she said. I was in such a dither to get home."

Rayne leaned forward eagerly. "Tell us about it. It is possible that he is an impostor."

She frowned. "Now you're frightening me." Her hair danced as she looked back toward the port companion-way, then back to Rayne again. "He was waiting in the taxi when I went out and he said he was Brother Perez." Her hand stole to her smooth ivory cheek. "Do you suppose…"

"In this part of the world," said Fang Gat, "anything can happen. You will, however, be protected. Mr. Cantey, here, is of the United States Government. I am but a private citizen, but you are assured of my complete support."

"Thank you very much," she said, but she spoke to Rayne, making his heart thump heavily. "I hope we're all wrong."

Rayne leaned forward seriously. "Miss Barstowe, I think you should be prepared for the worst. We overheard something between the Captain and Perez that doesn't sound very good. Be prepared, be as calm as you can, and remember that we are here to help if you need it. Perez is no Brother."

She went pale and swayed the least bit and Fang Gat's hand streaked out to steady her. "Easy on, child. It is better that you be prepared. Have courage."

She pressed her fingertips to her face and breathed deeply. She shook her head until her hair swished softly, then looked up. "I'm sorry. I'm afraid I don't have a lot of courage." She smiled tremulously. "And not a great deal of religion. Now it would seem that I will need both."

"For what purpose?" said Perez crisply as he came around the corner of the deck house. Taneeta shrank away from him, while Rayne noted satisfaction in the man's eyes. Perez gripped her painfully by the arm and almost swung her off the deck.

"Go to your cabin, and stay there," he snarled, but the snarl dissolved into a spray of spit, enamel and blood as Rayne, a scarlet balloon of fury bursting in his head, sent a rocketing left smash full in the man's mouth. Perez struck the deck on his shoulder blades and skidded into the scuppers where he lay stunned, but not out.

Fang Gat pulled the girl up against the deck house. "Stay here, little flower, so that no heels may bruise your petals."

Perez came up slowly, spitting fragments of a cheap bridge, blood, and Portuguese oaths. He raised himself halfway to his knees and said to Rayne, "For that blow, dog, you will this night roast in hell." From beneath his black alpaca jacket he drew a thin blade and leaped suddenly. A hard shod foot driven with furious force caught him just beneath the sternum and the knife described a weak arc, stuck up in the hard wood of the deck, then fell slowly to one side and lay glittering impotently.

"Brother," breathed Rayne as he wiped sweat from his eyes. "I've seen some *savotes* in my day, but that one took the cake. That kick would have split a lard barrel."

"His belly is quite soft," said Fang Gat, twisting his foot experimentally.

"He's quite soft all over," said Rayne bending over. He examined Perez carefully, than raised up. "In fact, he's quite dead."

Fang Gat made soft tutting noises. "I shall have to be more careful next time." He turned just in time to catch the girl as she slid down in a dead faint. He motioned with his head. "You'd better take her, Rayne. You're not armed. I am."

Her body was firmly soft and the feel of it in his arms sent a thrill through Rayne like a deluge of ice water. He started down the deck but the captain stepped out of his cabin and stopped him.

"What goes on here?" he asked harshly.

"Perez tried to manhandle the girl," said Rayne, preparing to drop the girl and defend himself. "I laid him in the scuppers and when he came at me with a knife, my friend kicked him. I'm afraid he's dead." He didn't have to drop the girl and defend himself; instead a huge smile split the captain's face.

"Well, now, ain't that a damn shame and him bein' such an accommodatin' fella and all that...the damned rat." Granger walked to the corpse and took something heavy from an inside pocket. He held up the bag and grinned wider. "Five hundred pounds," he gloated. He bent forward again and took out a thick pad of bank notes. "Five hundred pounds. No use lettin' good money go to the fishes. Hey, you, Tiki, throw the bastard over the side!"

A muscular Kanaka approached, stooped, picked up the body and heaved it easily over the side where it fell with a muffled splash.

As Rayne put Taneeta in her bunk, he inadvertently slid her skirt up and the sight of her leg in its golden ivory glory stung him hard beneath the breastbone. He wet a towel and mopped her face until she showed signs of returning consciousness, then he pulled a rickety chair up close and sat down.

"What..." She passed both hands over her face. "I must have fainted. Oh!" She reached down and covered her thigh, her face losing its pale hue in a hurry. Her eyes were damp with tears and accusing. "Did it come any higher than that?"

"No." His voice was so soft that it surprised him. "No, my dear, it didn't. And suppose it had? I didn't intend to do it and not for all the world would I attempt any disrespect of you."

She nodded and bit her lip. "I think I knew that. It's just that—oh, the devil." She sat up. "If my body is sinful and a temptation, and evil, then why isn't it ugly?"

Rayne sat back a little, feeling a little seared by the violence of her speech. "Who said it was sinful, Taneeta?"

"My father said so and sent me to a convent because I kissed a man. At the convent they made me pray that no evil would ever come because ... because ..." She held her face in her hands and cried a little. When she held her head up, a great aching throb went through him. It was a thing of such breath-taking beauty, so young, tender, miserable, defenseless, and confused that he cursed silently any creed that held beauty as evil and put such things into young impressionable heads.

He touched her hair gently with his hand and felt her flinch beneath the touch. "If beauty is evil," he said profoundly, "then there is no life nor any purpose in life. If your loveliness is evil, then let me be evil with you because I prefer it to anything else."

"Oh ... Mr. Cantey ..." Her hands went to her face in the same adorable gesture she used when she was confused or amazed.

He came back to the present with a rude jolt and leaped to his feet. "Better rest a while," he said brusquely. "And remember, you're not to worry about a thing."

He left her, feeling her eyes on him and cursing himself for a sentimental fool and an idiot. What had he said? He shook his head and shoved the thought out of his mind. Something fatuously noble and silly, no doubt. Something stickily storybookish. He almost growled as he came out on deck. He walked swiftly to his cabin and put on fresh khakis and donned a light jacket— after fitting his shoulder holster comfortably in place.

"I think I should have carried her after all."

Rayne jumped like he had been bitten by a *krait*. "What the hell, I didn't see you there." He looked at the .45 in his hands and flushed. "I'm still startle-conscious." He put it back under his arm.

"I'll say you are. I'm no slouch, but I wouldn't have been able to get my hand on my gun."

Rayne flushed again and sat down. "As a wag in Bureau used to say, 'There are two kinds of people, the quick and the dead.' I'm still alive."

"Don't brag," said Fang, chaffingly. "Who knows what the morrow may bring? Say, I used your first name a while ago. Sorry."

"You go to hell, you slant-eyed, hard-footed devil. You'd better learn how to use my first name."

Fang grinned. "What happens now? Granger has his money back."

Rayne stood up. "Better come along with me. I might need you."

They found the captain standing by the rail, spitting into the South China Sea with an air of proprietorship.

"A word with you, Granger," said Rayne, stepping in close to the captain and lowering his voice.

"Spit it out. I got other things to do with my time."

"I thought I'd tell you that I talked with British authorities last night at Kuching. They know you have Miss Barstowe on board."

"You ..." Granger backed up a couple of steps. "How the hell did you talk to them?"

"That big black bag of mine. Battery, short wave. I would see that she gets there safely, if I were you."

Granger was not as put out as Rayne had expected and sneered at them. "Why don't you see to it?"

"I shall," said Rayne, and in some manner there was a heavy Colt's automatic pressed lightly against Granger's belly like a pencil poking a Lister bag. Rayne smiled, hefted the gun and made it disappear beneath his arm with a quick whipping motion of the wrist. "Just in case you're in some doubt, chum." Having put a bit of bleach on Granger's plum-colored countenance, he walked away, followed by Fang.

"He could toss us to the fish tonight," said Fang as they emerged from their cabin where they had taken their after-dinner smokes.

"He could, but he won't. Murder is a somewhat messy business, even off Palawan. That's what lies over there to port just under the moonrise, isn't it?"

"How do I know? Or more to the point, how do you know?"

"I have a patent log in my head. We've been making something like eight knots and according to my calculations, we should be about there. I can see some lights on the horizon."

"If that's so, then we should be changing course before too long."

They did in less than an hour and by that time they were quite close to the southern tip of Palawan, entering the Sulu Sea.

"And now," said Fang with a chuckle, "anything can happen."

Taneeta came toward them in the moonlight like something out of a crazily exotic dream. She was dressed in something soft and white that the breeze plastered against her, pointing up the smooth graceful slide of her thighs beneath its folds. It, too, was cut low in front and the swell of her breasts made Rayne's throat dry.

"Feel better?" he asked inanely.

She smiled a trembling little wraith of a smile. "Much." She turned to Fang Gat. "I saw a man killed this morning and now it doesn't seem to matter."

Fang declined his head. "To anyone as bountifully endowed as you, only life matters. Death is a sick man's nemesis, the refuge of the coward, and the reward of evil."

Taneeta let a little laugh gurgle in her throat. "You sound just like a storybook Chinese."

Fang sighed. "It is the cross of all Chinese. They must appear mysterious, all knowing, diabolically clever, and full of wordy proverbs. In the flesh they are usually somewhat disappointing."

She held them both impartially under the spell of her eyes. "I may never get the opportunity of properly thanking both of you. Brother Perez was not Brother Perez. In his luggage there was a clipping and his picture. He is wanted from Cairo to San Francisco. In his description, it says he often impersonates a priest or a clergyman."

"What are mere thanks compared to the joy you afford our eyes?" breathed Fang Gat.

"Look," put in Rayne. "Don't I get a chance to make a few gallant remarks?"

"You let rice grow between your toes." Fang Gat threw Rayne a keen glance. "The hinges of your well-oiled tongue have become unaccountably rusty."

"Why," asked Rayne pointedly, "don't you go to bed and get some sleep?"

Fang moved away from the rail. "No wit is so starved that it cannot see the sun come up. I shall go and treat my fatigue with that balm which soothes all sorrow."

Taneeta pouted at Rayne. "Now my champion is gone. He says such lovely things."

"There is no rope of pearly words that can do you justice," he said with an exaggerated bow. "I would fain be whipped by you in preference to the most ardent caresses by any other woman."

"You do well," she said, "when Fang Gat is gone." Her face sobered. "Rayne, have you ever been caressed?"

"A little," he admitted.

"Was ... did you like it?"

"Certainly."

She sighed deeply. "I never have been. My father is a hard man who smites sin hip and thigh and can find more of it to smite than anyone I ever saw. He tried to put long white clothes on the natives, but they soon got dirty and the commissioner made him stop it. They caught all sorts of skin diseases."

"What about your mother?"

"My mother is a mixture of Chinese, English and Dutch. She isn't very demonstrative. Is it wrong that I feel hungry for some-one to love me, to hold me and ..." She shuddered and stopped.

Rayne knew that she had been thinking about such things a great deal.

"If it's wrong, then let's be wrong and love it ..." He stopped, suddenly appalled that he had practically invited her to a caress-ing party, but she didn't seem to have heard.

"I used to pet the little natives but Father said they were dirty and that I shouldn't touch them. The commissioner's son kissed me when I was fourteen and I almost fainted. I can't describe it."

"Was that when your father sent you to the convent?"

"Yes."

"And how old are you now?"

"Eighteen."

He gasped silently. Eighteen! She seemed older in some ways and completely adolescent in others, and no wonder. Her whole life had been constantly tyrannized. Never had she done what her own hungry nature demanded—but she had imagined!

The moon rose higher quickly and turned her from a beauti-ful desirable woman into a nymph of such unearthly loveliness that the cool wind could not keep Rayne's brow from beading with sweat.

"Rayne."

"Yes."

"Do you think I'm beautiful?"

"I think you're the most beautiful girl I ever saw."

She touched him on the arm. "You meant that. I know you did. You're being very sincere, aren't you?"

He felt foolish, but couldn't afford to show it. "Of course, Taneeta. In this moonlight you... you're just simply not real. You're like something someone dreamed up."

"I know," she said, not taking her hands from his arms. "I've dreamed so long and there never has been anything but the dreams." She shook her head and her eyes filled with tears. "Would you think it terribly forward of me if I asked you to kiss me?"

For a moment he was garroted with emotion. When he could command his voice he said, "It would not be the least bit forward, Taneeta, because you and I will always tell each other everything. Remember that. Everything."

She nodded soberly, like a child. "I'll remember, Rayne. Please kiss me... not like a parent, but like a lover."

"Taneeta... I daren't. It wouldn't be safe. You're in my blood... I couldn't be responsible."

"What could happen?"

He allowed a pregnant pause, then said, "Everything."

Breath fluttered into her throat. "I don't care," she whispered. "I can't live with me... all caged up like this. I'll go crazy. I can't, Rayne, I can't..." She fell against him and wept hard for a while, then held up her lips to him, her face inches from his, tumbling all his resolutions into a pile at their feet. Her face had a classic purity that sent a leap into his nerves and hardened every muscle in his body. Her breasts as they pressed against him were globes of hot ecstatic punishment and her loins seemed to burn him. Her lips were parted expectantly, palpitant from eagerness, and the red tip of her tongue flicked their surfaces.

He seized her face in an excess of passionate gluttony, letting soft hair fill up the interstices between his fingers and then, bending with torturing slowness, his lips touched hers lightly, and sank deeper into their honeyed embraces. A shock flickered through her body and a ragged song of hunger long dammed seeped eagerly from her throat.

Minutes later, he could see her face in a halescent blur and he realized that he was scarcely conscious. So frightening had been the assault of her touch upon his emotions that he felt weakened and almost ill. Never in all his life had his equilibrium been so sorely assaulted.

"Rayne ... Oh, Rayne, I can't be wrong ... You love me ... Tell me ... tell me."

"No ..." he croaked hoarsely. "No ..." Putting her away from him, he took four fast steps away from her, then he turned back. "I'll take you to your cabin, Taneeta."

A wall of fear, remorse, and impotence avalanched down on him. She'll hate me now because I haven't the guts. I'm a grown man with intelligence.

He stole a glance at her and saw that she was walking in a state of rapturous indifference. The tongue ran across her lips again as though tasting their recent victory; then she and Rayne were at her cabin.

"Lock your door," he directed, "and leave the key in it. Let no one in and scream if anyone tries to get in."

She nodded mechanically and turned her face up to him. "Thank you, Rayne. I love you ... so much that my heart seems smothered."

He touched her lightly on the shoulders. "You're starved, Taneeta. What you feel is physical."

Her eyes gradually focused as his words sank in. "But Rayne, what other kind of love is there?"

He opened his mouth, closed it, remembered some of his own stout arguments on the subject and shook his head. "Good night."

"Good night." She swayed forward and before he could move, her lips had covered his. They stayed there for one clinging, wildly sweet instant, then they were gone. And so was she. The door closed in his face.

"Tum tum de tum, tum tum de tum," sang Fang as Rayne stumbled through the doorway, his eyes still glazed from the awful impact of the girl's lips. "The words are my own," quoth Fang happily, "but I believe Wagner wrote the music. It is used …"

"Oh, quiet. I'm trying to think."

"Submit that any thinking done in present state of mind might be a waste of time."

"What sort of state of mind?"

"That in which, no doubt, a certain crimson smudge on your lips plays a part. She is naive and young, but she uses lipstick."

Rayne scrubbed his lips and took off his clothes to sit naked in a chair. "It will happen tomorrow."

Fang nodded. "So it will, or so I think. What about the course now?"

"Still going East. We're over the tip of Celebes now. At this rate we'll wind up in the Sangis or Talaurs or even down around Halmaheira. Once in that area—Lord help us. There must be all the islands in the world down there. The Moluccas, Wahai … islands all the way from Talaur to Australia and a million of 'em not big enough for any regular ship traffic."

"Nice thought."

"Thing is, he knows we're armed. He'll be backed up all the way to the crow's nest when he makes his move and all we can do is wait and hope." Rayne wrung his hands. "And if that weren't enough, I go take a fall for the girl." He could not know that he was being prophetic.

"A sad time," said Fang in a low voice. "He won't let her go with us, and if we don't go, we get killed."

"If I had a sub-gun I'd take on Granger, the crew and four more," snarled Rayne distractedly.

"We have no sub-guns. We have one ancient Mauser and one Colt. Moreover, we have another purpose for staying alive."

"The hell with it," said Rayne doggedly. "Right now you have no idea how far our 'purpose' is from my mind."

"I think you say that because what will happen to us will not be entirely disconnected with our goal. Usually, as the chronicles have it, saving the girl *and* the box would be impossible. We'd be faced with a 'choice' and love and nobility would chase each other around a stump until some fortuitous twist saved both our souls and the girl and all would be well."

"Fang Gat, nations will fall, men will be murdered, children starved and old people put out in the cold long after you and I are dead."

"What good would the girl do you," asked Fang softly, "if, for instance, you had no place to take her but China?"

Rayne stood up and rolled into his bunk facing the wall and did not speak. Fang Gat sighed, turned over and tried to sleep.

CHAPTER FIVE

"THIS IS CERTAINLY the day," said Fang Gat with something like grim humor as he held up his holster. The Mauser was gone.

Rayne dug frantically beneath a pile of his own clothes and came up with his holster also empty. He sat back with a groan. "Plucked like a fat fowl. Plucked while we slept and we knew he'd do it."

Fang Gat shrugged. "What good would weapons do? Alive we may achieve something; dead we could do nothing."

Rayne's gracefully powerful body tensed into ridges of taut conditioned muscle. "I'm trying to think what life will be like on an island with the *Lena* sailing away with Taneeta to a fate which writers used to say was worse than death."

"Get dressed," advised Fang Gat, "and try to put a curb on yourself. At the worst there will still be vengeance."

"And I'll get it," breathed Rayne, his hands tightly clenched at his sides. "I'll get it, Fang. Hear me? I'll get it."

"And I," said Fang Gat slowly, "will be pleased to assist."

All that day they were in a nest of islands. As the sun went down, they approached a small one with a single hog back of a mountain with a sharp peak at one end looking like a beheaded chicken.

"Okay, my wise friends. I hope you'll like your new home."

"Granger," said Rayne, his voice cracking from the strain, "if you so much as harm a hair of that girl's head, no ocean on this earth will be big enough for you to hide in."

"Hurt her?" Granger laughed lecherously. "Why, I'm gonna give her lovin' like she ain't never heard of. I wouldn't harm her the littlest bit."

Taneeta hurled herself from her cabin and into Rayne's arms before anyone could stop her.

A Kanaka moved to pull them apart, but Granger said, "Let her alone. We got time yet. Then when they're ashore, we'll have fun and she'll forget him. All these half breed women do. What they like is for a man to bruise 'em about a bit."

She clung to Rayne, sobbing, making his burden, already overpowering, well nigh unendurable. Only Fang's hand on his shoulder steadied him and drove out wild suicidal ideas.

Help came, briefly, from an unexpected quarter. The tall Chinese whom no one had noticed much appeared, holding two small bright revolvers in his hands. "I shall require that you and your men drop their arms at once." But he got no further. A thick-bladed knife thrown from the crosstrees thudded sickeningly into the tall man's neck and he stumbled forward, both guns going off, aimed with one last furious effort at the nearest Kanaka. Both bullets went home and the brown man rolled to the deck.

Rayne drew a long shuddery breath, feeling weak and sick deep in his stomach. His right hand, gripping Taneeta, ached and failed to translate the convulsive shudders that shook her.

"Over the side with 'im," snarled Granger, "and lower the dinghy."

A Kanaka, at a nod from Granger, caught the girl by the arm and tore her from Rayne's grasp, sending her sprawling on the deck, her round, glorious legs bared to the waist. She fetched up against the deck house half stunned, exposing the uncovered length of her beautiful body and, as Rayne went mad, there flickered idiotically across his tumultuous mind something Fang Gat had said when they first saw her: "… doubtless nothing under that, either."

Forgotten was the science of fighting, forgotten in a flood-tide of primordial savagery that carried the Kanaka to the deck beneath him. His hands, like iron claws, crushed the man's tracheal cartilages like pretzels and it took three hard, scalp cutting, blows from Granger's revolver barrel to topple him off, bleeding, to the deck.

Granger, panting and spattered with blood, wheeled to Fang Gat who leaned casually on the rail, his eyes narrowed against the smoke from his cheroot.

"Awright, you damned slant eye—ready for yours?"

Fang Gat shrugged expressively. "Restraint is a virtue never properly revered by Western civilization. Regrettable."

Granger growled furiously and tried to help the man on the deck to breathe, but the brown face grew blacker and blacker, the body thrashing wildly about, until finally the captain callously let him strangle and turned to the two men in the dinghy.

"Take 'em ashore," he ordered. "After that I don't care what you do with 'em."

One man lowered Rayne over the side by one foot, letting him fall the last three feet into the dinghy; then, drawing a cheap Spanish automatic, followed him and sat in the bow.

On the way to the wide white beach, Rayne sat up groggily, held his head in his hands but said nothing until the bow of the dinghy grated in the sand. "We're home," he croaked and burst into a cackle of hysterical laughter.

"Hold hard," said Fang Gat quietly as he helped him over the side of the boat. The gunman, seeing them go over the side, also slid over and went back toward the stern to help hold the boat and to place himself out of range of any attack. As Fang Gat passed the oarsman nearest the bow, he saw that the guard wasn't looking, reached out and struck the man what seemed a fly killer sort of tap at the juncture of his head and neck.

Holding his breath, he hurried Rayne out of the shallow water and hissed in his ear. "Run! Run like hell!"

Rayne managed to break into a shambling run, but before they reached the belt of forest, the small automatic began to speak from the boat. Fortunately, it was dark and the Kanaka was not a marksman even when provided with a good gun.

They huddled in the short brush at the edge of the beach until the creak of oars told of the departure of the dinghy, then they stood up and ventured cautiously out on the warm sand.

"Why'd ja wanna run?" asked Rayne thickly as he staggered and fell to a sitting position, whimpering as the jar set up a jangling cacophony of anguish in his head.

"I think I reduced the crew by another member," said the other, "unless my aim was bad. The soft bones crunched delightfully."

Rayne grunted uncaringly, then began to weep scalding, bitter tears as he thought of Taneeta. "Can't think," he mumbled after the paroxysm had abated. "Head ..."

"Come down to the water and let's give it a good washing. I wouldn't try to find fresh water in the dark. Salt water will sting but it will keep the wounds soft and prevent crusts from forming."

The salt water stung like all the ants of hell, but Rayne was so ill of body now that he was past caring and began to talk and laugh like an idiot. Back on the sand he vomited suddenly, then passed out cold, while Fang Gat sat near him, the red nose of his cheroot glowing in the damp darkness. It grew colder, so he piled sand over Rayne's outstretched legs and continued until he had covered him up to the chin. Then he sat silently beside him and waited.

Granger was furious when he learned that they had brought back a man with his neck cleanly broken and very dead. "Three men gone," he fumed, "all because no damned Kanaka has got enough sense to get out of the way. They gotta stand there and see how well they can take it. Well, three got it and three are dead." He looked in the faces of the others, brown, impassive, and blank. He cursed and bellowed. "Awright, up anchor and let's get the hell out of here. You, at the wheel, your new course is south by southwest on the nose. Hold it until I tell you different."

Blocks creaked as sail bellied out and the phosphorus glowed beneath the stern of the *Lena*.

Granger shaved himself that night and put on clean clothes, a pair of cheap silk pants that fitted his belly, buttocks and thighs tightly, and a once-white shirt, all without the formality of a bath. As he dressed, he swigged from a bottle of trade gin and chewed on the rind of a lime. His hair, wet, sour, and spotted with scabs from an infected scalp, he smoothed down with his palms, grinned at the mirror and went out on deck. His palms tingled as he recalled her nakedness when his man had hurled her to the deck. He licked his lips in anticipation of her soft virginal body and the wet passionate curve of her innocent lips.

"Open up," he said, toning his harsh voice down to a modest boom, "and let a real man into your life, baby." He waited, tensed to kick the door in, when to his surprise it opened and she smiled at him.

"Come in, captain."

"Well, now," he said roguishly, "that's what I call the ticket. No fightin', no hell raisin', just a nice friendly get-together." He went in and sat down on her bunk. "Baby, me and you're gonna have fun. I'm goin' to put you on an island where there'll be plenty of natives all bendin' the knee to you and ready to jump when you holler. Then, once every month or so, I'll drop by and we'll have fun. I'll bring you all sorts of clothes, baby, and there won't be nothin' you can't have. You'll see what it means to be good to Jack Granger."

She stood before him and for the first time he noticed that she wore a batik sarong that fitted her slender but generous curves, outlining the resurgent eagerness of her sharp breasts, the slimness of her waist and the slight arch of her stomach. Her eyes had been darkened about the lids by some cosmetic artifice and her lips were scarlet with paint. About her clung the scent of jasmine. He swallowed and held out his arms.

"Come to Jack, baby, and forget all the other men you ever knew."

She swayed toward him, but as she did so, a heavy jewelled comb fell from her hair and clattered to the deck under the bunk.

"Get it in no time," he assured her gleefully as he hopped spryly to his all fours. As he did, her hand flashed to a fold of a blanket and emerged with the blade Perez had drawn on Rayne. Her face was drawn and tight with determination as she clutched the long hilt with both hands and raised it over her head. With all the strength of her young strong body, she drove downward and the knife slipped in with such ease that the hilt thumped audibly as it stopped and the jar almost threw her off balance.

The helmsman was nearly asleep at the wheel when the dawn watch was changed so he was not as surprised as his relief who had stirred about a bit, drunk a quart of hot tea and now was refreshed by a cheek full of betel nut. The girl stood ten feet away and the manner in which she held a heavy Colt in her right hand, and an old Mauser shiny from care and use in her left, did not speak of side arms ignorance. The Colt nodded authoritatively.

"You, sleepy one, there. Take the wheel back." The man obeyed because authority was stronger than anything his sleepy mind was now capable of producing.

The Mauser nodded at the relief. "You go in my cabin and bring out the captain." Again she was obeyed mechanically, but with celerity. The Kanaka emerged from the cabin dragging Granger because he was too heavy to lift.

"Now call all hands on deck. No, don't go below. Just call them."

The seven Kanakas came from below, rubbing their eyes and asking questions that were effectively answered on the one hand by the body of their captain and on the other by the slip of a girl whose gun hands were as steady as rocks.

"Now hear me. Who has a gun?"

There was a silence for a moment, but there is one in every crew—the smallest and probably most tyrannized man, sensing emancipation, pointed. "One small gun belong Laota, mate."

"All right, Laota. The gun—drop it on the deck."

Laota, his face grim with hate, delved into the folds of his *lava-lava* and brought out the gun. But it came out shooting.

The girl's hands bucked as both guns went off simultaneously and the body of Laota was hurled back and spun about as he skidded on the worn planks of the deck.

She addressed the little man who had spoken and whose eyes were now round with admiration. "Take your foot and slide the pistol to me and ... No, just kick it ... There." She tucked her sneaker shod foot under the weapon and flipped it neatly over the rail.

Tiki, the bo'sun, who had seen the captain handle many a white man and woman, some not armed, some armed with knives and one with a pistol, squared his big shoulders and walked toward her. "Put'm down, please. Not nice for shootings people..." The Colt thundered, bucking her arm back. Tiki, on the verge of a charge, veered off and stumbled over the rail and did a cartwheel into the deep.

Her jaws were tight with determination and her legs were spread wide. "Any more?"

The little man, whose admiration had swelled to titanic proportions, knelt now and put his palms over his forehead; he bowed down to the deck. "Missy, captain. What Missy saying, we doing. My word!"

One by one the other men did likewise and Taneeta did not long tarry with orders. She turned to the man at the wheel, pausing momentarily as she realized that he might have crept up behind her, but not realizing that he had had just such a thought—her marksmanship had frozen him to the wheel.

She said, "Put the ship on the same course as going to the island where you left the two men. You savvy?"

"Me savvy," said the man eagerly, forgetting that he had stood a twelve-hour watch and was supposed to be sleepy. The way he spun the wheel was that of a fully refreshed man.

Rayne's superb physical condition came to his rescue and aside from a headache that behaved as long as he did not overly exert himself, he felt very good, all things considered.

Fang Gat, stripped to his shorts, had shinnied up a cocoanut tree and shaken down a sufficiency of green nuts at that stage when the milk is sweet and slightly carbonated.

An hour and a broken pen knife blade later, Rayne disinterred his knowledge of cocoanut husking and after a search found something that would answer for a husking stake. After that there was no problem about reaching the nut proper. They refreshed themselves with the milk, then stuffed on the jelly-like meat, after which Rayne felt even better and went into the water to wash his head, stoically accepting the fiery bite of the salt.

"What sort of place have we been marooned on?" he asked Fang.

The other laughed. "This is an insular needle in the haystack of Oceania. The United States Navy with a full carrier compliment might be forgiven for missing you here."

"Think it's inhabited?"

"Possibly. But cannibal natives are rare these days. There may be Dyaks here or Malays. In latter event there will be *proas* and paddlers to man them and we may be able to buy our way to Celebes, which I take not to be too far. Three, maybe four hundred miles, with plenty of islands in between."

Rayne sat down and let the rapidly warming sun drive the chill of the night from his bones. "Right now," he said nervously, sitting up, "I'd give this ten thousand bucks I have around my middle to be back on the *Lena* with a sub gun, chewing up

Granger's guts. I'd give another ten just for a little of that graven fatalism of yours."

"My fatalism in this case takes on the habiliments of reason. What, exactly, will fuming and fidgeting do?"

"They are the first throes of productivity. After one has fumed oneself out, then things have to happen."

"I shall be glad to join you in anything approaching progress."

Rayne got up and, turning his eyes from the sea, surveyed the dense cloak of jungle that hid the mountain and on down the hogback to the peak that looked dizzily high, but was probably no more than a thousand feet in altitude. The entire island was matted and tangled with a perfect hell of growth, with the inevitable fringe of cocoanut, sago and cabbage palms in the lower areas and fringing the beach.

"Why are cocoanuts always near the beaches?" he asked absently.

"They probably never get any further than a wave or a cocoanut crab can carry them. Nature has to do the reseeding, you know."

Rayne sat down again and fought off a wave of blind fury as Taneeta in all her soft virginal appeal drifted before his eyes. Something like a groan must have escaped his lips because Fang put a sympathetic hand on his shoulder.

"The dragon of circumstance has wound himself about you. Think how it would be if she were available and her parents stood in the way?"

Rayne shook his head. "You, with your age-old reverence for the heads of the household, bowed and stepped out. I'd have ridden the Sierra Nevadas down getting her, no matter parents, Boys Scouts or the National Guard."

Fang Gat chuckled. "I think you would. There was something wonderful about the way you went berserk and in the face of guns and knives tackled that Kanaka. When we left the ship he was in the last stages of asphyxiation. I wonder why Granger didn't kill us. It wasn't compassion, I'm sure."

Rayne frowned. "Nor robbery. I still have my money. Maybe he feels that unnecessary murder is an unnecessary risk. Kanakas might talk or the word get around some other way, and there was the girl. He might figure that by killing us he'd never take her except by force."

"He'll never take her except by force as it is. You would think he could see that."

"Maybe he does and doesn't care. One way or another, he'll take her."

Rayne got up and walked away down the beach.

They searched the island carefully during the day and found it approximately three miles long and one mile wide at the broadest point. There was neither harbor nor any sign of native life, except an old fire site on the eastern point near the needle-like mountain. For some reason, they gravitated back to the spot where they had been put ashore.

"Probably because we unconsciously expect a boat to come from that direction," explained Fang.

"I guess so," agreed Rayne as he slumped in the sand. "I feel dull and achey and tired and those mangos aren't sitting well on my stomach."

"We ate too many. I, for one, am not accustomed to a fruit diet to the exclusion of meat and rice."

"Me either. Tomorrow we'd better begin foraging for birds' eggs, wild yams and such. Are you much of a fisherman?"

"There will be shell fish, I think, and I know the good ones."

"Yeah. I had some training on foraging during the war. I can make a good fishhook from a sea shell."

"What'll we use for a line?"

"We could make one from our clothes, but I think I can still make sennit. I learned how in Samoa. You make it from cocoanut husk by pounding out the pith and using the fiber."

The sun sank into the Pacific in a bath of blood; like a gargantuan mass of lava, it seemed to cool along the edges and blacken the clouds, deepening the reds and bringing out the startling aquamarine blues of the sky. Gradually the reds deepened and blackened until at last there was only an angry glow that paled into the leaded dinginess of the clouds.

"A tropical sunset," said Fang Gat with a curious tone to his voice, "reminds me of a woman—passing in a few minutes through the stages of life."

"How?"

"At first she is young, fragile and virginal, then she deepens into glorious colorful womanhood. As time passes she becomes a woman of the lights, garishly, untastefully painted, too brilliant and somewhat cheap. Finally, there is a slattern clinging to her pitifully faded rags still plying her trade as best she might, dying and eaten with disease until the blackness of oblivion claims her."

"That's the artist coming out in you."

"A man," quoted Fang Gat softly, "is an artist the moment he imagines and long before he reasons."

Rayne turned about to face the impassive Fang. "Say, you really have a mood on, don't you?"

The other smiled. "The remark is not mine. Croce said it."

"Fang Gat, I am beginning to know you a little."

"Is that good?"

"You have no idea. I find that you are a sympathetic, sensitive man, and something of a philosopher."

"That's characteristic of the race. The Chinese, in order to get any enjoyment out of life at all, has had to live with his poverty and poor lot. His fatalism and his philosophy have been his salvation. Fatalism, however, is not a matter of race and neither is a philosophical outlook. Circumstance has made it the lot of the Chinese, as well as other peoples who are enslaved by environment or rulers. It is a sort of mass rationalization, or, should I say, compensation."

Rayne stretched out in the sand, closed his eyes and rested in the gathering gloom. "I hadn't thought of that. I suppose a serf back in the middle ages would have been fatalistic and a philosopher."

"Certainly. Otherwise he'd have gone mad. It is true that the Anglo-Saxon has in his blood the restlessness and energy to rise up and smite the tyrant, and so has the Chinese. The Reds are in temporary control, but even now they are opposed by some million guerrillas and bandits. China, in the truest sense, has never been really united except against the Japanese."

Rayne nodded, feeling too tired and sore both mentally and physically to continue the discussion. A moon as big as a hogshead and passionately illuminated poked a sickle of an eyebrow over the forest-padded hogback and looked down on the beach.

Rayne rolled over on his stomach and looked up at it. "A million women are giving it away under that moon," he said, his voice hoarse with futile pain. "And another is having it taken from her and is probably being beaten half to death as thanks ..."

"That's what you think," came a voice from seaward and Rayne leaped to his feet with such violence that he filled Fang Gat's eyes with sand.

"Taneeta!" Fang Gat pawed at his eyes, unable to see, but thrilling to the core at the sound of Rayne's voice. When he finally could make them out, they were clenched close and Rayne was murmuring broken endearing phrases as he stroked her hair with a hand as gentle as a nun's. Though his words made no sense, there was no question about the earnestness of his voice or the near hysteria of occasional sobs that came from his throat.

The girl's eyes were closed and her breath came deeply, relievedly, as she allowed him to caress her. Her body was soaked with seawater and her flowered print dress clung to her curves like wet paper.

"Suppose you two break it up and let's have some explanations," suggested Fang Gat reasonably.

Half an hour later, she made an adorable gesture with her hands, "So that's all there is to it. I killed him with the knife Brother Perez drew on you and I made the Kanakas throw him overboard. I had to kill two of them to make them understand that I meant business. They sailed me back here and I jumped over the side and swam in."

"Then…" Rayne put a hand to his aching head. "You mean they've turned tail and left us stranded here?"

Taneeta's smooth brow wrinkled then she began to sob. "I didn't think of it, Rayne. I suppose you'll hate me, but I couldn't think of anything but getting off the boat and getting back to you. I'm so sorry I did it. There's no telling how long we'll be here…" She put her head on her knees and wept. Rayne put a hand on her head.

"That's all right, darling. You're a very young girl and you did marvelously. Not one woman in a million would have had the guts to kill three men and make the rest sail you back here. You did the best you could."

She raised her head. "Rayne, you called me darling…"

He reached over and lifted her lightly across his lap. "I love you," he said, his lips inches from hers. "That's why I did it. I love you and I nearly died thinking about what was happening to you."

She sighed flutteringly and pulled his head down until the shock of her lips rippled through him like a current. Maybe she was young and sheltered, but her nature needed only a little suggestion and the sweet fire of her tongue made his head roar like a storm at sea.

Fang Gat, with infinite tact, wandered away from them and built himself a small fire some hundred yards down the beach. Rayne, seeing the glow of it from the corner of his eyes, shook himself free of the drunkenness of emotion and caressed her arms. She was cold.

"We'll have to get you out of those clothes, darling. You'll freeze."

Her smile was tender and carried a certain suggestion of belligerence that he understood when she spoke. "It is sinful for a woman to undress before a man. I have no other clothes, Rayne. You know how that will leave me if I undress."

On the ship he had felt restraint and even a touch of shyness, but now that was gone. Such things made no difference now.

He nodded and smiled. "It'll leave you naked. If you're beautiful when dressed, naked you'll be a goddess and I shall bow down to you in worship. There's a little pool where a stream comes down from the mountain. We'll go there and wash the salt off you and then we'll build you a little shelter of some sort. In fact, we'll build that first, then wash you off." She pressed herself close to him for a moment, then she kissed him with such sweetness that his heart seemed to be one vast ache in his breast.

He led her a little way into the jungle to protect her from the wind and there, where a *toi* tree spread its wide roots protectively, he made a little shelter of tree branches and lined it with ferns and soft grasses. Over the tops of these he spread broad banana leaves, then stepped back and examined his handiwork.

"Is it big enough for two?" she asked, her teeth chattering a little.

He nodded dumbly and took her in his arms again. "Now let's go wash the salt from you and your dress. I'll build a fire here first, though, and your dress will dry while you sleep." He built a roaring fire and when he had banked it high with branches, they walked back to the beach and started for the fresh water pool. It was a round hole in the rock, worn deep by the waterfall that poured over a low cliff some thirty feet high. At one end there was a strip of volcanic pebbles, but the end near the waterfall was deep and cold. They went to the deep end and sat on a flat rock near the water's edge where Taneeta took off her sneakers and socks, then turned to him.

"Rayne, you aren't afraid to love me?"

"How do you mean?"

"I mean...I'm young and I'm not very smart. You're the very first man who ever kissed me like that." Her eyes filled with tears. "I know I'm young and not worldly and all that, but I do know I love you so that it makes me ache and I can't seem to kiss you hard enough or hold you tight enough to make it stop. I'm about to pull off my dress and then I'll be as naked as I was born, but somehow just because it's you, it seems all right. I don't feel that I'm doing anything wrong. It doesn't seem that anything we would do could be wrong."

A sensation of smothering assailed him again and he shook his head, trying to clear it. When she spoke or looked at him, he seemed to lose his balance and poise, swimming in the warm wet wine of her attraction that seemed to emanate from her like a palpable vapor.

"Nothing we do is wrong," he said, his voice ringing with a richness that he hardly recognized.

She smiled and there in the moonlight, she lifted the damp dress by the hem and skimmed it over her head. This time she wore a white mist-thin silken underthing that clung lovingly to her hips, but that was the only thing left. She looked down at him for a moment, standing proudly erect, her chill-hardened breasts making conical shadows down her white flanks. Then, with almost ritualistic slowness, she divested herself of the filmy briefs. Again, she stood for him to admire, then she turned and let herself into the water, feet first. She didn't stay in very long because the water was so cold, and as soon as she had washed her hair and dress and flounced around for a moment, she swam to the edge of the water where Rayne stood transfixed with paralytic admiration and gave him her hand.

With a surge, he brought her out on the rock, dripping crystaline drops and lovelier than in his wildest dreams he had ever imagined. With a strangling sound, he drew her wet slippery body close and from her cold lips that warmed almost instantly, he took full measure of her sweetness. She wept for a moment when he released her and started to put on her dress, but he interposed his coat.

"No, don't put that back on. Use my coat. It'll warm you up."

She shrugged into the coat, then came back to him, her eyes wet and serious. "Rayne, I don't want to be warmed that way."

"What ... ?"

"Love me." There was a musical sob in her voice. "Love me warm, Rayne. Take me and hurt me with love. We can't stand it any longer. I can't stand it any longer."

She was right! Why let this absolutely unparalleled situation go on any longer whan they ached for each other with a madness that would only get worse?

He cupped her chilly face in his hands, then tilted it to the white light of the moon. "Let's go to your shack where, once you're warm, you can go to sleep. Here, take my pants too. I have on shorts." He took off his pants and made her put them on and rolled up the legs for her.

She stood wistfully looking at him until he was through, then said, "I wish you didn't have on the shorts."

There was nothing he could say, so he kissed her again and they started away from the pool toward the warmth of the fire.

They squatted before the fire that had burned down to a big bed of coals and hung out the dress and briefs. Rayne replenished the fire and soon they had to stand back from it. In the firelight his bronzed hide and long rippling muscles made Taneeta shiver.

"You're lovely, too, Rayne."

"What? Oh ... hell." His skin turned red and she let go several notes of tinkling laughter.

"Rayne?"

"Yes."

"I'm warm now." It had come and even after he had told himself that it would have to happen, he still shrank somewhat as the time drew near.

He stood up and she came into his arms again with a satisfied sigh. "Let's go in the shelter."

There was plenty of room inside and Rayne, spreading his shirt out to give additional protection from stems and rough spots, saw his coat fall beside him. "Spread that out, it'll help. And these, too." The pants fell beside it as an icy thrill chased up his spine. Then she was in his arms.

She was warm now, her skin soft and faintly fragrant, the points of her breasts pricking his chest, their firm globes spreading a little and telescoping into wide areas of tremulous sensation. Her lips were soft and hungry, even as her arms and body were strong and avid. Her hands found buttons and stripped him bare, the trilling little sound coming again to her throat as his lips rained kisses on her body and his hands caressed her flesh.

Words came shudderingly from her very depths. "Oh, Rayne. Oh, God, I love you … I want all of you completely … all … mine … mine!"

She was a soft avid serpent in whose nature had always been the book of Eve from the pages of which she drew all the knowledge of the ages. In Rayne she raised a kind of trembling terror at the unbelievable ardor and performance, the exorbitant demands, and the stupendous response that she was able to extract from him.

Later, they lay comfortably lax in the deep rapturous silence and quietness of their little bower, pervaded by a nutrious fog of clean healthy woman, a far sweeter incense than man could ever synthesize. Her stomach moved in spasmodic jerks, feeding her starved lungs with needed air and his hand touched it with gentle reverence.

In the darkness he could feel her eyes on him and he knew that they were wide with wonder and placid as pearls. Their mouths met and clung, not with the hard savagery of passion, but with the gentle gratitude of utter and complete satiation.

He stroked her hair that was dry now and as soft as silk to his touch. "I love you," he said simply.

"I love you," she returned. "Forever and always."

"Taneeta, suppose you get pregnant?"

She wriggled ecstatically in his embrace. "Oh, Rayne, wouldn't it be the most wonderful thing in all the world?"

He subsided and a chuckle jerked his diaphragm briefly.

CHAPTER SIX

FANG GAT TAPPED on the shelter roof with a switch. "I think you two had better get up and see what I've found in the dawn of a new day."

Inside, the occupants jerked guiltily, then Taneeta smiled. "I'm not ashamed, Rayne. Not in the least."

"Hell, I'm not either." He drew on his clothes and stepped out to toss Taneeta's dress to her. "What have you found?"

"Come look while she dresses. We'd better hold a council of war."

They stepped out on the beach and Rayne saw that the *Lena* was anchored almost in the same place she had been when they were put ashore. The dinghy was coming in, oars flashing in the pink blush of the early sun.

"Well, what do you know," breathed Rayne. "I have a pocket knife, but that's all."

"I have one also and there's no question of running."

Rayne shook his head. "Nope. That'd never get it. We'll know in a minute."

The dinghy came steadily on and soon her nose grated in the sand. The small Kanaka stepped out and walked toward them, the Mauser and the Colt stuffed in his waistband, showing plainly.

Rayne stepped forward. "What do you want?"

The little man stopped and almost wriggled with embarrassment. "We coming ashore, picking up passengers b'long boat. Missy she swim chop chop last night. Not cricket! Would brought her along dinghy very eassy. So sorry. Very fine woman." He drew the two weapons and advanced, extending them to Rayne. "Bring pistols b'long you, mebby Malay, mebby Dyak."

Rayne took the guns mechanically and turned a blank face to Fang, handing him the Mauser. "What do you make of this?"

"You, fella boy, him name what?" asked Fang.

"Naming Tanala. Very good boy. Wheel, diesel, making sail. Very good boy, my word."

"What now fella marster b'long you? Granger dead!"

"No fella marster b'long me. No boy gottem fella marster b'long him. My word!"

"Granger dead," repeated Fang, "boys going where, doing what?"

Tanala shrugged generously. "My word, what fella boy him doing now? Granger dead, no pay." He spread his palms. "You making good fella marster b'long schooner. You say, fella boy him do."

Fang Gat turned to Rayne. "It looks like we are now the owners of a schooner, complete with crew, if a somewhat bob-tailed one."

"Well, I'll be damned," said Rayne, his head buzzing with the sudden turn of events. He faced Tanala. "You boys want to work along for us?"

Tanala nodded and grinned widely. "Okey dokey, plenty good. You, him, good fella marster. Never cuss boy, never whip boy. American fella marster me knowing b'long Mindanao b'long war. Top hole fella marster."

Rayne stuck his hands in his pockets. "Is that the way the rest of the men feel?"

Tanala bobbed his head again. "Making talk along me. Him fella boy happy Granger dead. Fella boy bad like Loata and Tiki, dead, b'long shark belly, my word. Missy ..." He broke into a peal of delighted laughter. "Whattawoman. Goddamn!"

Rayne grinned. Tanala's last words certainly branded him as an erstwhile associate of Americans.

Taneeta came up and Tanala fell forward in the sand, his forehead on his palms. "Missy safe, b'long fella marster. Okey dokey. My word."

The *Lena* seemed fairly to skim the waves as she sliced through the water, apparently taking a certain exuberance from the fact that her command had changed and her crew was happy. This last was attested to by the song that now filled the ship, something Rayne had not heard when Granger was alive. The crew members worked hard and willingly because Rayne had promised them no brutality and double wages. Taneeta they treated with the awestruck respect they would have accorded one of their pagan goddesses. Her slightest wish was law and the steward, who doubled as cook, even strove to tickle her palate with dainties.

The sun was setting in a display of chromatic extravagance that even surpassed the previous night's effort. Taneeta stood watching in the bow with Rayne. She was dressed in white twill shorts and a scarlet silk shirt that the wind molded to her every line as though it had been made of elastic. Her face was serious and her hair in its heart-shaped bob lent her face a certain pristine purity that sent the choking ache to Rayne's throat again.

"What's troubling you, darling?"

She sighed. "Rayne, I'm afraid there's going to be trouble with my father. He's a fanatic, a demon, when he gets angry."

Rayne tightened inwardly. He hadn't considered that angle. "Well, what shall we do?"

She faced him, her jaw hard. "Don't take me home, Rayne."

"But—"

"There are no buts. He wants me to go to school in Britain or Australia as soon as God overcomes the beast in me—so he says. Then I'm to marry properly which means some stiff upright member of L.M.S. and come back to the islands and spread the gospel." Tears were making trails over her cheeks. "I don't want to marry an L.M.S or spread the gospel." She came close and held him with trembling strength. "I want to be your wife and bring you fine, healthy children whose lives will not be squeezed into tiny dreadful patterns."

He patted her shoulder. "It's all right, darling. We won't take you home yet. Maybe we can reason with him when I do. We'll get married as soon as we can and you'll stay with us until—" As he stopped, she looked up quickly. "I have no idea," he went on, "how long or where it will take us."

She sighed and snuggled closer. "That's all I want to hear. Just so I can be with you. Nothing else matters. Thank you, Rayne. So very, very much."

On the third day away from their prison island, they sighted a body of land.

"Celebes," said old wrinkled Koa, spitting a stream of blood red betel juice expertly toward the rail and watching the wind take it over the side.

"What port are we near?" asked Rayne.

"Ketong."

"It's not on the map," said Fang Gat, seeing the look on Rayne's face.

"How big is it?" asked the latter.

Koa shrugged. "Little much, not very big. Big boat no go along Ketong. Lighter take'm in cargo. B'long man—Voort."

Celebes, at this spot, was not the sand-fringed gem they had left. Ketong squatted in a heat-ridden half circle opposite a mangrove swamp that seemed impenetrable. There was a rickety dock and a sheet iron warehouse and a scattering of tin topped "bungalows" and native huts.

Mynheer Voort, a fat Dutchman, appeared to be in a state of collapse on the verandah of his store, bar, dwelling, with only the casual movement of his palmetto fan attesting to life. His dingy ducks failed by some three inches of coming together at the belt and his navel looked out at the heat with a blind sweaty eye. His head was naked, except for a circlet of colorless hair that still struggled for existence, appearing much like a descended halo about his immense head.

Rayne stopped at the verandah steps. "Mynheer Voort?"

Voort opened one eye and moved slightly. "Ja, coom in poys und sid down. Vhat could I did for you?"

They took the indicated chairs and, after examining them for scorpions, sat down.

"I could use a cold beer," said Rayne, mopping his face.

Voort's button of a nose wrinkled. "*Coldt* beer! You is an American."

Rayne nodded. "American, hot, thirsty, and looking for a little information."

Voort turned and shot a stream of Malay at a boy who was wiping off table tops inside, then he sat back and appeared to go to sleep, except that his palmetto fan kept moving gently as though to assure that the cooling effects were not overcome by the effort—which is a science one develops in the tropics.

Rayne surveyed that part of the sky line that the trees didn't cut out and saw the tremendous peak of Latimodjong glimmering like a monstrous tooth in the distance. From some distance out at sea they had been able to appreciate what was in store for them in the way of broad plateaus, mountains and the unbelievable turmoil of jungle.

"At least," murmured Fang Gat in a voice that reminded one of Voort's fanning, "there are no tigers and things here."

Voort opened one eye that oddly resembled his navel and spoke. "Ja. No beasts to run you opp a tree, but—" He shrugged off the other dangers.

The boy came out, bearing two lime coolers filled with crushed ice and floating several lime rinds. Rayne accepted his eagerly and over his tall frosty glass Fang Gat's eyes gleamed appreciatively.

"This is really something," said Rayne, when his drink was half gone. "You can tell the boy to make two more and maybe another two before I'm done."

"Too much is giffing cramps, poy. Be careful."

"I'll take the chance. Now, about the information—"

This woke the fat man up and he leaned forward. "Information I haff little off in this place, as you can see. Prices of cocoanuts, indigo, nutmeg. Such dings like dot."

Rayne leaned forward. "I'd like to know how to get to Van der Vanter's rubber plantation."

Voort's face congealed into a mass of expressionless suet and his mild eyes were blank windows. "Dot," he said at length, "iss strange."

"Why?"

"Dis iss a small port. Nottings off der important, you see. Yet in two monts three peoples iss asking directions to der plantation off Van der Vanter. Iss strange."

"Let it be understood," put in Fang Gat smoothly, "that we wish the gentleman no harm. In fact, our business has very probably no connection with him at all."

"Dot," said Voort, stolidly, "iss even stranger."

Rayne sweated faster and sucked at his ice, wondering just how hard this was going to be.

Voort heaved mountainously in his chair and squinted out where a rain squall had hidden the *Lena* from sight.

"Strange also is der *Lena* coming in under new ownership. Sooch I assume since Granger vas alvays der first in to der bar."

"It's a long story," said Rayne tightly. "I'll tell you if you insist, but I'd rather not."

Voort nodded pleasantly. "Der Kanakas could haff did it. I alvays told him he vas too rough mit his crew."

Rayne was silent and Voort was evidently fascinated by the sweeping tendrils of rain advancing on them. Finally, he said, "Der rain blows on der verandah. Should ve go inside und continue der exchange off information?" He smiled and heaved himself up heavily and waddled into the interior building which was dim and cooler than the verandah.

The rain came down with a whooshing roar and in a second all landmarks and even the trees were blotted out in a pall of water. For five minutes it drummed deafeningly on the tin roof, and almost as it came the rain drifted on southward, leaving things dripping but little cooler.

"Now," said Voort, lowering himself into a creaking chair, "shall ve continue?"

"Yes," said Rayne, "you were telling us about Van der Vanter."

"Ja, so I vas." He nodded and sank back in the chair. "Very strange."

Rayne, quelling the nervous fidgets with an effort, finished another lime cooler and crunched a bit of ice.

"He's dead," said Voort suddenly.

Fang Gat resembled a snake waking up. "Dead?"

"Ja. Dead! Sold der plantation, vhich vas not rubber, by der vay. He planted many things and dug for odders."

"Such as?" Rayne was tense.

"Goldt, diamonds."

"Gold, and diamonds in Celebes?"

"Ja, ja. Mines even. Goldt mines." He shut his eyes again, then opened them. "Do you vant Van der Vanter himself?"

"No," said Fang Gat. "There was a man on his plantation we wanted. That is why we are here. We know nothing of Van der Vanter."

"A white man?"

"We're not certain."

"Ah. Ve get places quickly." He leaned his head back and closed his eyes.

Rayne dug out his wallet. "Mr. Voort, if you will look at this I think you will understand why I can't tell you as much as you would like to know."

The big man opened one eye, then the other, then sat erect with a speed he had not shown before. He took the wallet and studied it for a moment, then looked up. Gone was the lethargic man who seemed about to go to sleep. "I'm sorry, gentlemen. I didn't know."

Rayne, who had intended merely to impress, was curious because he had done a better job than he had intended or even thought possible. "What, Mr. Voort, didn't you know?"

The other tapped the card in its plastic window. "Dis card. I know off a man who carried one."

"Who?"

Voort's alert eyes clouded over and became blank windows again. "Vhat can I tell you?"

"Tell us about Van der Vanter."

Voort clasped his hands across his stomach. "Vell, he vas a hard man, an ambitious man. Planting and trading vas not enough. He made much money, he spent much money. At vun time he had seven women in his house, none off dem vhite. Den dere vas a vhite woman, blonde, from a UN mission. Der man vas infatuated mit her und quit visiting. For a year no vone saw him. Den came der udder man."

Fang Gat seemed strung on a tight wire. "A man?"

"Ja. I neffer saw him before. You see, Van der Vanter alvays used dis port, for reasons off his own and sometimes at night. I did not ask qvestions because vunce ve are friendts. Ven der man comes, not long later comes vord dot Van der Vanter iss dead. Und der vord dot dis blonde voman vas his vife und dat she inherits. She sells, und oudt she goes, mit der man, through Ketong." His eyes narrowed. "You vill forgiff me, gentlemen, vhen I am reluctant to talk. You see, Granger took dem avay."

Occasional drops fell clatteringly on the tin roof and the beaded bamboo curtains rustled gently.

Fang Gat relaxed and laughed softly. "As long as a man can be surprised, life is worth living."

Rayne mopped his face and smiled. "We'll be doing some doubling back, it would seem. Mr. Voort, do you know where they went?"

Voort shook his head. "Only vhere dey told me dey vas going. Und because on my map der man he makes a mark to be sure I know der location perfectly, den I am suspicious."

"Can you show us?"

"Ja. Coom, please."

The office was a seldom used collection of spindly furniture which Voort's bulk had bent considerably askew, dusty ledgers, an ancient desk and windows whose panes were flyspecked into translucence. He drew out a map and peeled it carefully open out of respect to the blobs of mildew that looked like circles from wet glasses.

"Vhere you see der red circle." He pointed a pudgy finger. "In der Banda Sea, der island iss a speck."

Rayne tore a piece of paper from an old yellowed magazine and measured the distance. "Airline from here something like five hundred miles."

Voort shrugged. "Vhy don't you ask your Kanakas? Dey vas dere."

Rayne blinked once, then a smile spread over his face and he hugged Voort suddenly. Voort backed away for a step or two, his face blank with amazement.

"From the mouths of sedentary traders come the words we love to hear, sir," said Fang Gat. "My friend is an impulsive man."

Voort nodded vaguely. "But it is much too hot. Let us go back in der bar."

As they went in a man came through the doorway. He was as thin as a rail, but he carried himself with the same Bond Street air with which he wore his grimy whites and the hand-plaited hat of palm frond.

"I say," he said, screwing a monocle that had no lens into place. "Frightfully sportin' of you to ask me to have a drink."

"Nobody asked you," said Voort bluntly. "Und you can't half any more here."

The boy—he was scarcely more than that—flipped his hand casually. "Very well, I'll take my business elsewhere. I say, chaps, you wouldn't have room for an extra hand on the lugger, would you? Nauseatingly healthy and all that, in spite of my bones. Right now a drink would put the pip back in my squeak, if you'll pardon a pun. Rum fella here, this fat, overbloated Dutchman, who let the tropics get him and now that they've cut his allowance off, he won't give a man a drink. No sportin' blood."

Rayne felt a peculiar thrill. "I'm Rayne Cantey and this is Colonel Fang of the Nationalist Army."

"Percy Oldwick." He shook hands with them, his eyes steady enough but red, and his face cut with bitter, yet whimsical lines. "Army man, myself. Called Perc, mostly. Bunged about here and there after the war while jolly old Winston and jollier old Franklin muddled the peace. Army wins it, politicians lose it. Getting to be a bore after a few thousand years. Did I hear some one say something about a drink?"

"I'll stand them," said Rayne, still in the thrall of his strange feelings. "What'll it be?"

"Er—small scotch and a little water. And Voort, please put in a little ice. Met some Americans at Sidney. Affable chaps who had found that the way to beat the heat was with ice. Chinese invent tea, we ruin it. Scotsmen invent scotch and we make swill out of it. But it is still a festive tipple, the drink of temperance. Ever hear of anyone getting stinko on scotch? Indeed not. No one with a taste for it wants to stun the taste, so he generally starts out on scotch, then pops over to gin or something cheap unless he has lashings of money." He popped his monocle out and caught it deftly in mid air. "Either you chaps have lashings of money? If so, I'm temporarily embarrassed and might ask for a small advance if I get drunk enough to lose my good taste." He blew on the empty monocle and polished the imaginary glass on his coatsleeve. "Nuisance, this," he muttered, "but dash it, I can't see a bloody wink without it."

Rayne wanted to laugh, but he felt a strange pity for this scarecrow with his elegant air and silly chatter. "What about a double? A single of scotch isn't much."

"What? Oh, quite right. Can hardly taste one of Voort's singles. Did you say a quad?"

"That's all right. Make it a four-timer, Voort, and don't spare the portions."

They sat at the tables with scotch and water and the more Perc drank, the more affable he became. "Coincidence, meeting you chaps. Fancy what a small place the world is. Why, it can't have been many years since the war was over and in the war there were a million Americans. I must have known a thousand myself." His face fell and he sagged. "But I hardly think we met though, did we?"

"It is possible," said Rayne, kindly. "I was all over doing this or that."

"Don't say? Well, I was doing that mostly with the boys in Burma, too. Met that general Johnny of yours ... what's his name? Gad, what a man. No rest for any of them. Drive, drive all day and night. Jungle—you can have it. That's why I'm here instead of the jungle." He smiled sheepishly. "Hell of a jungle out back. Pig sticking is topping. Fierce bastards with tusks like knives." He took a drink. "Ever meet a chap name of Moak?"

The silence that fell was thick, but it took a while for it to filter through Perc's somewhat befuddled consciousness. He looked at Fang Gat, then at Rayne. He lifted one eyebrow, then the other. "I say, did I say something wrong, perchance?"

Rayne said, "Do you know Moak?"

"Rather! Bounder, he is. Got me out here on some wild goose chase. Something to do with sapphires or emeralds or diamonds or some such baubles. Took the last fifty pounds I had. Sure thing, you know. Disappeared, left me here in Voort's hotel and a few months later, after I had lost my pride sponging and had even worked a little, he affected not to know me. Threatened to have me jailed. Imagine that. Never saw me before, he said, but that wasn't the way he talked when we were at the Gilt Pheasant in Singapore. Got passage with a lump of a native in a converted troop landing craft and here I am." He peered at them. "I seem to sense something. You don't know him, of course."

Rayne put a hand on the man's sleeve. "I could use another hand on my schooner and when we've finished our mission, I'll stand you passage home, or wherever you want to go."

Perc's pale, starved nose twitched as he looked first at one of them, then the other. "Shockin' sight, I must be," he croaked, his eyes filling with tears. "Dirty … crumb … no pride anymore …" He swallowed painfully and dashed the tears away, but more flowed. "Not—" He choked a little. "Not havin' a cruel joke on ole Perc, are you, chaps? Don't know …"

"No," said Rayne, gently. "I'm not joking. We'll be glad to have you along."

"Creepers …" His hands trembled as he lifted his drink and some of it slopped to the table top. "Jolly sportin' … just fancy ole Perc shakin' the mud of Ketong." He shook with silent laughter. "When are you shovin' off?"

"As soon as you get back with your duds."

"Duds …" He laughed again. "Have another set of whites for Sunday. Fearfully religious ole person, you know." He laughed again. "I'll go get 'em. Be right back." He got up and walked out of the door with even more insouciance than when he entered.

"Dot vas a kind gesture, Mr. Cantey," said Voort. "But der poy iss no goot."

Rayne shrugged. "I've seen that kind before, Mr. Voort. Did he come here in that shape?"

"No. Dot I must admit. Vhen he came he vass a nice poy."

"Then I think when he leaves he'll be a nice boy. Does he owe you anything?"

Voort lifted his fat palms. "For vhat you are about to do, could I do less? I vipe out his bill."

"That's kind of you. I see him coming at a run, so we'll get along. I really appreciate your help."

"For vhat it iss vorth, you are velcome. Dere is one thing more. Bedder you vatch out mitt dot man. He iss not der sort I'd trust too far."

"You mean Perc?"

"Ach, nein. Perc is harmless, iff a little cracked in der knot. I mean Moak. Der one vhat came through here mitt Van der Vanter's vife."

CHAPTER SEVEN

THE *LENA* SHOVED her blunt bows through the water as comfortably as a housefrau kneading bread for the week's baking, her course south by southeast. There were several islands in sight, and old Koa stood by the helm, his eyes lining up landmarks and watching like an eagle for white water.

Perc, now almost fastidious in his Sunday whites and a very passable sennit hat, came up to Rayne who was standing by the rail and watching the porpoises play and the frightened flying fish swarm up from the deep.

"Spoke to one of the crew johnnies about Moak," he began. "They remember him well and that little island he told Voort about. He's not there."

"Yes, I know. I spoke to Koa about it. He says they put them ashore at Neita, but I can't find it on the chart."

"They're all supposed to be on the chart, but if they had 'em all there it would look like a potato bin. Some that are off the standard routes they don't bother. Now, if you had a Navy chart ..."

"Yes, but we don't. But Koa says he took a sighting and he can find it again."

"What's there?"

"Small island but some fairly large buildings. Koa says it was once the summer playground of some sultan and was deserted when the sultan fell from grace or was assassinated or something."

"That'd be the place for Moak, all right."

"Who's the woman?"

"I don't know. She's a puff, over on some UN business. She ups and flys the coop and takes up with Moak after her husband pops off. Name of Marlene. He calls her 'Deit.' Big, fine-looking blonde with a body that'd make your hair curl—and the way she throws it around! Bitter twist on her face, though. Like she was disappointed in love or something. He, naturally, comes in on all Van der Vanter's plantation brought and I'm told it was considerable." Perc squirmed and looked embarrassed. "Frightfully good of you to pick me up like that, old boy. Can't thank you enough."

"Then stop trying." Rayne grinned. "There's just one thing. Miss Barstowe is spoken for. I saw you eyeing her yesterday."

Perce flushed to the roots of his taffy-colored hair. "Rum! Sorry about that. Can't help saying, though, she's a looker. Don't know when—didn't mean anything, though. Sorry. Rum ..."

Rayne laughed. "Hell, you needn't perish at my feet. Any normal man would have noticed her."

Perc averted his face and laughed with him. "Women—nothing in my young life. Boudoir buccaneer of sorts, but nothin' serious. Never fear from ole Perc."

Fang Gat, who came up then, smiled and said, "Famous last words. Many a man has uttered them and failed in the clutch."

"Is that modern, or one of those fearfully sapient sayings of Confucius?"

"Modern, but not new. Few things are. I," he said, turning to Rayne, "have found the treasure trove containing six perfectly good Colt automatics—acquired some time ago from a G.I., of course—and a good two thousand rounds of ammo. Last, but not least, there are some thousand pounds in notes besides the thousand he paid and retrieved from Perez, as well as the gold sovereigns. Cute little stuffed cubby over there behind that dull lithograph of a barque under full sail on a purple sea."

"Granger's cache," said Perc hollowly, who had heard the story which had added considerably to his interest in Taneeta.

"The weapons might prove valuable," said Rayne. "Perc, can you handle a pistol?"

"Right ho! Quite well, in fact. Always practicin' on government expense, of course. Webley."

"Well, these Colts are service automatics. The most stimulating two and a half pounds of weapon you ever hefted. You might have to put your knowledge to use."

"Right along with you, chaps. After what you did, my best isn't good enough."

Tanala was standing by the wheel, singing in a reedy falsetto a song that dealt with the improbably lush properties of one Fui, the girl with the red hibiscus in her hair. Rayne, who was fairly well conversant with the various dialects of Polynesia, heard and was reminded that men are pretty much the same wherever they might have been born. By his side was Taneeta, her face almost ghostly in the starlight, the moon not having risen as yet. She wore a dress of soft silk that caressed her legs, sending up tiny tingles of sensual message.

She shuddered and leaned against him for a moment. "Rayne," her voice was low and vibrant. "I want you."

He drew her close, thrilling to the core of his body as her legs heated through their thin covering and reached his skin like a stimulating balm.

"I haven't said anything since we came aboard because..." she rested her forehead on his shoulder, "because I've always been such a proper thing. It would seem after that night on the island I wouldn't feel that way, but I do—or rather, I did. But it's stronger than I am, Rayne. I can't help it."

"I'm glad it's stronger than either of us. I wouldn't have lasted this long if there hadn't been other things pressing me for attention. One of them is exposing you to the dangers that we will certainly find when we get to Neita."

She clung to him hard, then eased her grip. "I don't care, Rayne. I want to be where you are—where, when night comes

I can come close to you and have your hands on me ... take my clothes away and have me for your own." She shuddered again and moved subtly against him, sending a blaze of passion skating through his nerves like an acid sting.

He kissed her hard and said in a low voice, "Go to your cabin, Taneeta."

"Will you come?"

"Yes, I'll be there shortly."

He went to his cabin and shaved; then he took a bucket of water to the stern, soaped down well, and made Koa sluice him down with the rest. Then he slipped into clean khaki pants and walked boldly to her cabin.

The small bulb sent forth a feeble light, but it was enough to see her stretched on the bunk like some fabulous Grecian sculpture. He went to his knees and slipped his arms under her and lifted her lips to his. She coiled about his neck and upper torso and her fragrant warmth sent him into that now familiar roaring chasm of emotion that made him another man.

Her hands moved eagerly, familiarly. "Please, Rayne. You don't mind?"

He looked at her through the red haze and shook his head. "No, darling. Nothing. I don't mind anything at all. Not when it's us."

Her sigh shuddered deeply and her eyes were despairingly entreating as he closed the distance and felt as though a switch of fire had been touched.

"I wonder where Rayne is," Perc inquired of Fang Gat.

Fang Gat's eyes were inscrutable, but Perc thought he detected a gleam of censure in them. "He is where he is for his own purpose," said the former, shortly.

Perc flushed. "Seem always to be putting my foot in it, but she didn't impress me as that kind."

"What kind is *that* kind?" The eyes were agate hard now.

"Er …" Perc's face was the color of a boiled lobster. "Well, you know…"

Fang Gat smiled thinly. "I'm afraid not. You tell me."

"Not the sort, that's all," Perc burst out. "If he's where I think he is."

Fang Gat was silent for a moment. Then he sat up on his bunk and teetered precariously on the edge. "Is your own past so spotless that you sit in judgment? For your own information, Mr. Oldwick, these two people were thrown together in circumstances which, to employ an understatement, were extraordinary. They intend to marry as soon as it is feasible. That they are of the metal that can partake of heights of joy before any such ritual is performed does not, in my mind, indicate anything but psychological stamina which I think you would never understand. If you are still in the thrall of the codes as put forth by Her Britannic Majesty, Victoria, then I feel it necessary to point out that you were picked up by the heels, so to speak, from rather a hole, in a state which I dare say would do little to bring luster to Britain's proud banner."

Perc stood up, suffering, his face almost purple from humiliation, but he saw no pity in the hard black eyes. "Sorry…" He croaked dismally. "Really sorry. Should have known … rum." He tottered from the cabin in a state of acute pain and Fang Gat sank back with a grim smile on his thin lips.

The *Lena* bounded merrily under full sail down through the wide mouth of the Macassar Strait, rounding the southern tip of Celebes and through the Gulf of Bone. Rarely were they out of sight of islands and as they drew into the Banda Sea, old Koa went on the alert and stayed that way. At his own request, he was relieved of wheel duties, whereupon he wandered about the deck, making innumerable trips to the chart room, squinted for long periods first at one smoky hump of island, then another, seemed to be counting and so conducted himself in general that he made Rayne nervous.

Fang Gat leaned interminably and nervelessly against the port rail and smoked his cheroot with such stoic calm that Rayne was further irritated. Perc, as nervous as a young bride, flitted here and there, cleaned weapons, smoked innumerable native cigarettes made of rank tobacco and banana leaves and laved his throat with water when it craved a much stronger quencher.

"What," asked Rayne at length, "is biting you, aside from your thirst?"

Perc started and giggled a little crazily. "Rum. Made a fearful ass of myself last night, really. Have no idea what got into me."

"How?"

Perc's face flamed like a Balinese sunset. "Must have been potted. Hadn't had a drop, really, as you know. Made a crushin' statement about you and the little girl. Should have known better. No business of mine … really." His embarrassment was pitiful and his face was drenched with sweat. Rayne looked fixedly at him, wanting to laugh, but conscious of a certain mild anger as well.

"To whom?"

"Fang. Got my blinkin' ears clipped for my trouble." Perc wriggled with mortification. "Had to tell you some way—make restitution and all that sort of thing. My profoundest apologies … in the dust at your feet and other such demeanin' gestures, dear old adventurin' person. Can't thank you enough for what you did, giving me a lift. Guess I'm a rotten sort of bloke to—" Perc mopped his face and whooshed out a tremendous gust of air.

Rayne smiled. "Forget it. I guess she sort of bowled you over and stirred up the St. George in you or something like that."

Perc laughed hollowly. "Don't deserve it, really. Been meaning to ask. What are we after, since this is no pleasure cruise, obviously, what with your questions about my ability with a pistol. No business of mine, of course, but I fancy you'd not mind tellin' me."

"That might be open to argument." Fang Gat had come up and now stood nearby, eyeing Perc with dispassionate steadiness. Perc blushed again and shuffled about on his sneakered feet.

"Rather. Of course. Neither of you knows me, do you now? Rum. Sorry, of course." He started to leave, then turned about, his flush paling and his blue eyes hard and steady. "Wouldn't be still holdin' my last night's *faux pas* against me, would you, dear ole Fang?"

Fang Gat shook his head slowly. "Vindictiveness is the sport of inconsiderable souls. It is a luxury I cannot afford. Let your mind be at peace on the subject." He turned to Rayne. "I bow to your opinion in the matter."

Rayne looked Perc over closely. If he were acting and for a purpose, then he had proven clairvoyance because too much had happened by the turn of fate, not excluding their landing at Ketong. Rayne shook his head. "Caution is always indicated, but it can be over done. Perc, we are after something we think might be very important to several governments. Ethically speaking, it belongs only to those who will make the best use of it. We are going to recover it if possible. We don't know what it is or anything about it except that it is highly important. So much so, that several men have been killed and more will be, probably. Governments, patriotic organizations and wealthy individuals are all scrambling for it. It disappeared from Hong Kong and we think it will be wherever Moak is, although that last we didn't know until we arrived at Ketong."

Perc's eyes narrowed thoughtfully. "Thanks, awfully—trustin' me like that. Now I can see why Moak wanted my fifty pounds." He looked quickly at Rayne. "What do you suppose the woman's doing in this?"

"I don't know. She sounds like an over-sexed opportunist and not very stable to go ducking her UN job, getting married, and teaming up with Moak."

"She's sexed enough by nature," said Perc. "Any amount over that would be a gratuitous surplus, to say the least."

"Well, we'll know before long. From the way Koa is sniffing about and muttering to himself, we'll be arriving before long."

"Hadn't we better have a word with the crew about this thing?" put in Fang Gat. "The offer of a good bonus might help keep them on our side. And after all, it is Granger's money."

"That would be a good idea, and since you make with the pidgin so well, suppose you tell them. Make it good. Seventy-five or a hundred pounds. Something that'll make their eyes pop. Give them ten pounds around now, just for good faith."

"I say," said Perc, "that's generosity."

"Another man's money," said Rayne grinning. "I can afford to be. You'll get a fat slice, Perc."

"I could do with one. You suppose we'll run into pecks of pearls, or some such stinkin' rich ole pot of good luck like in all the South Sea stories by that London bloke and the others?"

"Hardly. Too many people around now. You have something special on your mind?"

Perc wriggled. "Had thought of takin' a shot at sheep ranchin' in Canada. Have a gossy ole uncle there, name of Oldwick. Pater's frater. Frightenin' ole feller, though. Got all sorts of land and wants me for a partner when I can make a spot of cash and hold onto it long enough to get there. No cash, no Perc—that's the law."

Koa walked rapidly past them and gave an order to the man at the wheel, then he returned and pointed. "Making proper look-ing, guessing, counting. Come along island, one day. Seeing?" He pointed and dead ahead on the new course there lay three islands. One quite close, one some thirty miles away and dim in the haze, but latched in the notch of them, was a puff of pinkish cloud catching the rays of the setting sun.

"Which one?" asked Rayne.

"No one. No can see island. Under cloud. Bimeby mebbe see island tomorning."

"Tomorning," with the *Lena's* rigging and sails dripping dew and silver trails of it running crazily over the deck planking, they stood in the bow and saw the shark-teeth outline of Neita rising out of the early mist. She was still some twenty miles away, but as the sun rose, the naked rocks of her peaks showed wetly scintillant in places. By mid-morning they were skirting her northernmost point and could see her wave-washed beaches bordered with the ubiquitous coco palms. Back from the beaches and up the sides of the backbone of mountains, Neita was a tumbled mass of black green jungle with only the highest and rockiest of the peaks bare.

"About four times as big as our first island," said Fang Gat.

"Do you see any signs of habitation?" asked Rayne.

Koa thrust a pair of Zeiss glasses into Rayne's hand. "You mak'm looking along there, where white water."

About midway, the island there appeared to be an inlet or bay with the mouth protected by fangs of bare rock against which long rollers foamed into a broad belt of lather painfully white in the sun.

Rayne looked for some time and shook his head. "I can't see anything."

"Too far," said Koa. "What you telling man coming out meeting boat?"

Rayne turned and looked hard at the old man. "What do you mean?"

Koa shrugged. "Long time we b'long here. Captain, he tell man Moak *Lena* coming chop chop and pick'm up."

"Ahhh," Fang Gat spun around. "You hear this—ears b'long you?"

"Ears b'long me," said Koa with satisfaction. "Captain put'm down. Bimeby next trip pick'm up, chop chop. Long time we taking along Ketong, other island. My word, him mad, mebby. Him fella marster bad man—bad eyes."

"Nice," said Fang Gat. "He's expecting the *Lena,* but not us. What tack shall we take?"

"Pardon the interruption from a lesser man," said Perc, "but with me here and good ole Rayne also, he'll know ruddy well something's gone potty. Not much to do but see what happens."

"He's right," said Rayne. "He'll know me and what he remembers isn't likely to make him happy."

Fang Gat shrugged fatalistically. "Then I'm of the same opinion as Mr. Oldwick. Fortune has deserted us. Knowing you, he will instantly be on his guard and we stand to learn nothing."

Rayne bit his lip. "As I see it, all we can do is try to make a deal with him."

Perc gave a short barking laugh. "Christus, but you must have Wall Street backing you or else the U.S. mint. That's the only sort of thing that'd impress Moak. That lad has his peepers on a financial empire, not just a fat pay off."

"I wonder. Rather, I've been wondering about that tall Chinese who tried to rescue us. His only purpose aboard, I think, was to spy on us. Therefore, he wanted us to reach our destination where he would have suddenly discovered some pressing business at the same place. That's why he tried to keep Granger from putting us ashore. Now the thought occurs to me—are any of his people with Moak?"

Perc shook his head. "I wouldn't say so. He had five people with him, and no Chinese."

"Who were they, exactly?"

"The girl, and four servants. They were half breed Malays or something. Hard to tell just what. May have been some of Van der Vanter's children. He was mad for women of all sorts ... Easy on! I forgot. There was Van der Vanter's daughter, too. I forgot about her because I didn't see her, but Mynheer Voort told me she was with them."

Fang Gat raised his eyes. "Speaking of Mynheer Voort reminds me—he said that in two months three people had asked for directions to Van der Vanter's plantation. Counting ourselves as one and Moak as one, who do you suppose was the third?"

Perc shook his head. "Maybe it was one of the servants, but that's all they looked like—servants. There was one old Malay with one eye, but he could have lost that from trachoma. A lot of them do here. There was nothing to suggest he was anything else."

Fang Gat took the binoculars and looked toward land again, making a soft sibilant sound as he took them from his eyes. "We've cleared the headland. Take another look."

Rayne looked through the binoculars and gasped. "What is it?"

"Looks like a city of the lost Atlantic. Since we're in the Pacific, maybe I should say Mu."

Close in the curve of the tiny harbor, coming all the way to the water, were buildings that shone dully white in the sun. They had the compact shapelessness of some ancient eastern city where whole blocks were under the same roof or gave that impression. That it was very old and not the summer home of a small time sultan was attested to by the tremendous monoliths of rock supporting enormous façades that frowned out over the waterfront.

Rayne took the binoculars from his eyes and handed them to Perc. "What do you make of those buildings, Perc?"

After a long look, Perc shook his head. "Never saw anything to touch them, nothing like them any place. Reminds one of some Roman ruin that isn't ruined yet —and yet I know it isn't Roman."

"What's your guess, Fang Gat?" asked Rayne.

"In this instance, I think wisdom is contained in silence. I've seen Angkor Vat and this reminds me of it, but this is in a much better state of preservation viewed from this distance. It has evidently been kept up by some human agency."

"It gives me the creeps," said Taneeta, after a look through the glasses. "Not a sign of life about."

"Who," asked Rayne, "built Angkor Vat?"

Fang lifted his eyebrows. "That's a question neither science nor history can answer. There are inscriptions on it, the Feathered Serpent and other things that have duplicates in Yucatan. Ever read the *Popul Vuh?*"

"No."

"You should sometime. You'd see that there are many mysteries still unsolved. For instance, what is known as the Quiche Mayas settled in Yucatan and the Central American peninsula, bringing with them quite a high civilization. But the question is—from where? The Asiatic Indians are said to be Naga Mayas. It has been suggested that there are strong indications that Chinese and Japanese people are a branch of the Quiche Mayas and I do know that there are many places where they have found, once within reach of the Incas, fragments of character writing that, at first glance, would be taken for our modern Chinese or Japanese writing—to a non-student, of course."

"Then you think we may have discovered something?"

"I think it unlikely. This may be some ruins of that period, but they've been visited before, I'm sure. It is possible that the aforementioned sultan used the buildings for his summer retreat and maybe repaired them, but there aren't many things still undiscovered. Explaining them is another matter."

Rayne looked at Koa whose basilisk eyes were glued to the opening of the little bay.

"What do you think, Koa?"

"Thinking not too much good. No mans, no womans, no natives. Nothings. Too much nothings."

Perc bit his lip nervously. "Jolly well agree. Too damn much nothing. Not natural, you know."

"How long ago did you put the people ashore here, Koa?"

"Long time. Thlee monts mebby puttem people along island. Not good, too much nothings."

Rayne was irritated by indecision, something that was new to him; he was simply not used to it. But in this case, there was too much chance of making an error by precipitous action. He turned to Koa.

"Do you know these waters?"

"Pretty good knowing them."

"Then can we sail around the island about this far out?"

Koa nodded. "My word!" and turned to give the order to the helmsman.

The rest of that day they spent ducking in and out among shoals that boiled dangerously close to the *Lena's* sides, tacking, quartering, then finally sailing directly away from the wind. The water seemed alive with fish of every sort, from gigantic mantas to tiny jewels that flashed about the bow like aquatic butterflies. The sun beat down mercilessly, but by now they had become so accustomed to the heat that they allowed the sweat to trickle unnoticed and did not mention it, seemingly by tacit consent.

By sunset, they had reached a position opposite the little crab claw inlet and were again examining the weathered white ruins through powerful glasses.

"Making look careful along docks," said Koa helpfully. "Seeing if boats b'long Moak."

"That's an idea," said Perc and bent his glasses shoreward again, giving an exclamation after a bit.

"What do you see?" asked Rayne, coming to his side.

"I see what looks like the prow of a *proa*—you know, high and curved. Could be something else because the rest of the boat is hidden by a great stone piling. That's all, though, that looks like a boat."

Rayne turned to Koa. "Get the hook over the bow. We might as well get set for the night. Tomorrow morning we'll go on in regardless. We can't stay out here indefinitely."

"Water too deep," objected Koa. "Cable not enough long. Sailing on top of deep reef, anchoring there."

"Do it any way you want," said Rayne. "Just so you get us secure for the night."

He turned to Fang Gat. "Did you talk to the men about their bonus?"

The Chinese nodded. "They were much elated. Already at double pay they are talking about the wives they intend buying when they get back. I think they will be as loyal as they can be."

"Well," said Rayne, "that's all we can ask."

"Quite. In weighing loyalty one must take the personality and other things into consideration. They have a loyalty to self that comes first and after that they serve through affection, gain, and other fundamental drives. What do you think of keeping a watch?"

Rayne shrugged. "We're out about three thousand yards and we've seen nothing. But I'll leave it up to you."

"In that case, I shall set up a watch. I'll break it at midnight and put another on till dawn. It is true we've seen nothing, but to quote the excellent Koa, too much nothing. True, we are out three thousand yards, maybe more. But people in these latitudes think nothing of taking a trip of a thousand miles in a *proa* or outrigger."

After dinner, Taneeta came to Rayne where he stood alone in the bow, looking shoreward. "See anything?"

"No. I thought I saw a light several times, but I rather expected to think I saw a light several times. I'm surprised that I haven't seen other things in my imagination."

She came close, enveloping him in a warm vapor of some subtle fragrance that stirred him. She wore white shorts with a broad red stripe down the side and a little sleeveless jacket that buttoned closely across her stomach, leaving several inches of bare creamy midsection showing. Her breasts carried on a silent battle with the restraint that held them in.

"Rayne." She shuddered slightly. "I'm afraid."

"Of what, darling?"

She waved her hand toward the island. "That place. I don't like it. There seems to be a sort of evil coming from it like an invisible wave."

"You've been reading comic books."

She flushed and hung her head. "Not many. The sisters didn't like for us to read them."

He laughed and patted her hand, but she came into his arms, taking his gesture as full permission. She was soft and warm and tenderly appealing and Rayne, as usual, was putty in her hands. He was clad in nothing but khaki shorts and the feel of her curves pressed so closely to him activated his own arms. Their pressure squeezed a little sound from her and her hands roved eagerly over him. A rigor flitted through him and, oblivious to the calm stare of the man on watch to whom such things were nothing about which to excite himself, Rayne picked her up and carried her to her cabin.

Rayne was awakened the next morning with such suddenness that he roared out a protest and swept his hand toward his holster, but his eyes then told him it was useless. The holster was empty and standing before him with a piratical grin on his face stood a man whom he had seen before. He held a Luger in his right hand with a certain insouciant carelessness that was not carelessness at all, but superb confidence. He wore faded shorts, a holster and nothing else. He was blond and tall, his skin burned a red bronze, his hair bleached almost white by the sun. Rayne could hardly repress a twinge of admiration for the man, so cool, efficient and self possessed—but yet, as deadly and cold of heart as a cobra.

"Get up, old chum," he said, his face lighting up with a grin that was wholehearted if somewhat chilled by china blue eyes as hard as sapphires. "Get up and pay me a visit on my island kingdom. I wish to repay my debt to you—that slug in the shoulder. Remember?"

"It could have been through your heart," Rayne reminded him.

The grin widened. "Oh, quite, but you sentimental chaps are put to such an awful disadvantage by being so soft. You should have killed me, Cantey, because that is just what I'm going to do to you. But only after I decide just what form I shall choose to effect it. I wouldn't want that lush creature in Number One cabin to hear of it, though. She and I will make a perfect couple."

Fang Gat, who had been largely ignored and who had feigned sleep, chose the moment to come out of his bunk like a shot, but Moak's super-consciousness and poise was not affected. Pivoting like a dancer, he lashed out with the Luger and smashed the barrel along Fang Gat's head and had the weapon on Rayne again before the latter could spring from the bunk.

"Tut tut," he reproved mildly. "Such hospitality and you needn't look expectantly through the door for help, old bean. Everything has been taken care of with a minimum of fuss and bother. We saved you till last. So arise and greet the day. It could be your last, you know."

Rayne got up, slipped on a pair of fresh khakis and a crisp shirt, then went to Fang Gat's assistance. He had stirred a couple of times and moaned, but a dash of water from a carafe provided the needed shock and he sat up, feeling his head tenderly. He even had the spirit to smile up at Moak.

"May I congratulate you on your speed? I underestimated you."

Moak shrugged and grinned back. "Don't let it irk you. Others have underestimated me—such as the man who came to me bringing a certain little box of which I'm sure you gentlemen know nothing. He tried to hold me up, to make me dig deep into my—er, slender resources for an exorbitant sum. Instead, I shot him just below the sternum and took the box for nothing. Foolishly, he carried it on his person."

"What was in it?" asked Rayne in spite of himself.

Moak's laugh was liquid and ecstatic. "Since you're not interested, I don't mind telling you. It is something that governments and certain private individuals will give a great deal to recover. If I make less than a cool million from it, I shall be disappointed."

"And what," asked Rayne winningly, "if you get nothing but six feet of sod over your face?"

Again came the laugh that irritated Fang Gat to the point of almost losing his aplomb. "That, chaps, is something I wouldn't bank on too heavily were I you. Now come along. The sultan's launch will be waiting to take us ashore."

CHAPTER EIGHT

RAYNE WENT OUT first, followed by Fang Gat, then came Moak still wearing his wicked leer. Sprawled on deck with his belly ripped wide open—nothing but a *kris* could have made such a wound—lay the man who had taken the second watch. His limbs were askew and his neck seemed broken. Flies had swarmed over the body and Rayne could see by the dark congealed blood that Moak had indeed been careful and had taken plenty of time so as to prevent any outcry.

He pointed his Luger at a small beturbaned man who was nearly black. "You may take the gag from the woman, since there is no one for her to awaken now."

The little man bobbed his head and stripped a dirty rag from Taneeta's face where she lay crumpled against the deck house, clad in a pair of silk candy-striped pajamas. Moak picked her up and kissed her heartily.

"Have no fear, little dove. You will be well treated and by no one so well as me."

She slapped him with all her strength, but he only laughed and shook his heavy shock of white blonde hair. "Spirit, eh? Well, I like them that way, but they must also know something of discipline." He drew back a hand and slapped her deliberately in the mouth, knocking her to the deck.

Rayne's muscles tensed for a leap but the sinewy fingers of Fang Gat held him back. "Not like that. Remember Granger. We must not start a conflict with the odds the way they are."

"Where is the drunken one?" asked Moak of a man who stood stoically by in turban, loin cloth and little else, save a very efficient Schmeisser machine pistol.

"He in cabin now. Put'm there and lock door."

"Get him. By the way, Cantey, when did you start befriending beachcombers?"

Rayne, his lips white with anger, said nothing. But he held himself in hand only with supreme effort of will helped by Fang Gat's grip on his arm.

Moak shrugged and turned to Perc who was brought out in a state of befuddlement.

"What the hell are you doing here?" asked Moak in harsh astonishment.

Perc simpered foolishly. "Hadda collect my fitty pounds, old warlike fella, y'know …"

Rayne's lips curled with disgust at the sight. Where had he gotten the liquor? He still held a bottle loosely by the neck and, leaning up against the rail, he emptied it and sent it crashing into the *proa* that was tied alongside the *Lena*.

"Lettern gedda goddam bare feet in there now," exploded Perc as though he had set a booby trap that would decimate the enemy.

Moak ignored him and turned to his men. "Get up the hook and we'll take the *Lena* into the harbor."

The harbor proved to be almost round and the inlet was scarcely fifty yards wide, around which the breakers boiled with futile anger, but inside the bay the water was as calm as a lake. As they came closer, the ancient mass of stone took on a new hugeness and a solidity before which all the forces of nature and the ages seemed impotent. Atop all the walls were catwalks and little hutments that had housed warriors of a long dead past; back of the walls were the conglomerate arrangements of buildings so thickly collected that it could not be determined whether they were separate or compressed into one mighty edifice.

Along the waterfront were docks and stone pilings that might have taken care of the largest ship had she been able to navigate the narrow inlet. Huge stone posts showed where hawsers had cut into them from innumerable mooring lines. But the place did not suggest commercial use. It appeared more like the villa of some fabulously wealthy potentate and the waterfront structures were fronted like verandahs opening directly upon the water. The columns holding up the heavy roof were severely plain and without the ornamentation of Rome or Athens—they were there for a purpose. But the place looked more like a lake front resort than any commercially intended enterprise.

More little brown men came out on the broad stone-flagged street and, as the *Lena* came in to the dock, they grabbed thrown hawsers and soon had her made fast. They seemed all of a kind with loin cloths *pareo*-like about their middle, with a *kris* thrust cunningly through the folds of the cloth like the men on the *Lena*. They thrust the gangplank over the side which was useless, really, because the *Lena* was almost flush with the edge of the dock.

"Come ashore to the kingdom of Moak," he said, grinning in his infuriating manner. "Oh, Deit, come over here and view the captives."

As he spoke, a tall, marvelously curved blonde Amazon came between two columns and out on the quay where the little brown men were making the schooner fast and chattering in Malay. Her hair glimmered gold in the sunlight and her hips, under her batik sarong, swayed provocatively.

As she drew nearer, Rayne could see the sultry cast of her face, the sensuality of her deep blue eyes and her full moist lips. She was a little too seductively contrived for Rayne who had never seen so much pure sexual dynamite in one woman before in his life. She seemed to emanate it like a visible vapor and he could feel his stomach muscles contracting as her eyes rested boldly on his. They went to Taneeta and he could see the faintest curl come to her lips. She looked at Fang Gat and her face went almost audibly blank. For a long moment her eyes held his a flush darkened her fair skin and she turned away abruptly and walked back toward the frowning façade of the great building, losing in some manner the idolent sensuality of her walk.

Rayne cast a surprised glance at Fang Gat whose face resembled a teak woodcut, so utterly expressionless were the features. Fang withdrew a cheroot and lit it slowly.

"That," he said with the utmost calmness, "was Marlene, the blonde I told you about from San Bernadino."

Moak, taken up with supervising the docking operations, hadn't noticed the drama. He turned around and frowned. "Where did Deit go?"

"She returned from whence she came," said Fang Gat easily.

Perc tumbled from the *Lena* to sprawl flat and giggled as he sat up. "Something terribly amiss with my cuck—cordination." He sat crosslegged and began to make idiotic motions with his hands while singing in a scratchy falsetto, "Waltzing Home Matilda." Several natives grinned tolerantly, but they all left him alone and Moak seemed to forget him entirely.

"Come on and I'll introduce you to your dungeon. Marvelous dungeons these people had." He made them precede him across the flagged street and into the building into which Marlene had disappeared.

Inside, the mausoleum seemed even larger, with its lofty walls going all the way to a roof which was not there. Instead, there was an opening some twenty feet square that let in light and air. Along both sheer walls were narrow stone steps leading into dark holes which Rayne took to be either rooms or corridors leading to rooms.

"Not up there, cobber," said Moak, motioning with his automatic. "You go down, as I said. Dungeon, you know."

They did go down and it must have led to a level below the water because the floor was slimy and damp, but due to the hole in the ceiling above, which was a duplicate of the one in the roof, there was light of a kind. Along the walls were smoked niches where ages ago cressets had burned, possibly with tallow or nut oil.

Moak motioned them into the great apartment. "Now I don't propose to chain you because nothing less than an atom bomb could ever get you out of here, so don't waste your energies plotting escape. Such food and water as I choose to send you will be lowered by rope from above, so there will be no need to open the door. What, by the way, became of Granger?"

"The sharks have him," said Rayne, with some satisfaction.

"So? Well, no matter. All I wanted from Granger was his schooner and I intended that he rot here—" He stopped. "Why not? Why should I soil my hands with you when all I have to do is take my people and depart? Of course the rats might get bad, but if they do, then you'll have food ... until they get you."

Moak stepped back through the portal. "Well, pleasant dreams, souls. Have fun and all that."

"What," asked Fang Gat, "have you done with Mr. Oldwick?"

Moak looked blank for a moment. "Oh, you mean Perc." He laughed and shrugged. "The last time I saw him he had found a bit of string and was having the time of his life with it. I shall probably take him out beyond the reef and toss him overboard as we leave. He was a nuisance once, but he has deteriorated so that he doesn't even irritate me any more. He amuses me."

The thick door turned on silent stone hinges and finally crashed shut, fitting the wall so neatly that from a distance it could hardly be seen. A mad laugh sounded from above. They looked up and saw Perc on his knees near the opening, pointing his finger and shrieking with laughter. Rayne clenched his jaws and turned away to sit on a long slab of stone that had been fashioned into a bench.

Fang Gat smiled tightly and sat beside him. "Careful artisans, these ancients. Think of a place that would last in this climate, even if it is all stone."

"So that was Marlene?"

"That," said Fang Gat, after a slight pause, "was Marlene and if you remark how small the world is, I shall be moved to strike you."

"Who cares?" retorted Rayne. "Rotting here is a pleasant thought. Let's case the joint." Inch by inch they went their way around the immense expanse of wall, tapping and examining the joints of the stone that had been so cunningly cut and set.

"What did they use for mortar?" asked Rayne.

"You haven't seen any?"

"No."

"They used none. These stones are so wonderfully polished to size that you couldn't get a knife blade into the interstices. I'm wondering if this room is below the water level. Since we entered the first floor at some eight feet above water level and then went down forty feet to this level, I should say we are some thirty odd feet beneath water level."

"What difference does it make?"

"None. I'm just wondering how they managed to keep water from seeping in here. It is damp, as are most cellars, but by rights, there should be enough water in here to support the *Lena*."

Rayne leaned back against the huge stone support that rose to the ceiling. "Well, here we are. Taken like a bunch of school kids. We had a watch, but he either went to sleep or was sneaked up on. We should have all stayed awake."

"Or we should have sailed away and come back," said Fang. "I can think of any number of things we should have done. Thing is, we didn't do any of them and here we are."

"We should have pulled some magnificently clever coup," said Rayne bitterly, "like they do in fable."

"I'm afraid there is no fable about this," said Fang wryly. "I will wager that this is a more immutable sort of fact. I may not be in a dungeon built by some lost race, but I'd bet on it."

"And poor Perc," said Rayne sadly. "He cracked up like a dropped bottle. I knew he was wandering near the edge, but I didn't know how near."

"The chasm between sanity and madness is not as wide as is often supposed. I am thinking that we really know very little of Mr. Oldwick. He revealed to me before we were surprised that he held women in high esteem—old worldish, as it were. His esteem is built on that rather naive British and American fiction that women are something just a little above what one expects the mortal human animal to be. Such impressions nurtured to the highest degree from infancy can produce quite a disillusionmental shock, if you will pardon a clumsy word. I rather think that Mr. Oldwick was shocked when he learned that you were attending Taneeta in her cabin. Since she is manifestly young and pure and innocent without any of the so-called brands on her body or countenance, it was hard for him to accept that she lent herself to any such assignation. Such is the inevitable lot of men reared in such a manner. They sleep with harlots or women of easy virtue, then marry someone who resembles their mother in some remote way, not so remote to them at the time, and find that successful coition is almost impossible, both by virtue of their attitudes and the girl's background which hardly admits that such women are even equipped for the meaner obligations of nature."

Rayne smiled faintly. "With me down here and Taneeta up there, I feel on the verge of going mad myself. I rather suspect you of talking windily to ease my mind."

"Then you must think I have a low opinion of your mind. You talk to me and see if it eases mine."

"What do you feel toward Marlene?"

Fang Gat shrugged philosophically. "What purpose would a feeling of mine serve one way or another?"

"We are not discussing purposes," snapped Rayne. "You loved her once, and not too long ago. Do you or do you not love her, now that you have seen her in—what we might call her shame?"

"I find that hard to answer," said the other, carefully. "You see, Rayne, you are crammed to the ears with some of the very same sort of environmental impressions as Mr. Oldwick. I truthfully find the question very hard to answer."

"Then you do love her. You still love her, in spite of what she has done. In spite of everything."

Fang Gat didn't answer, but Rayne could see his face set in cold graven lines.

"Maybe I shouldn't have asked you," said Rayne, contritely.

The other shrugged. "Who knows? Is a man despicable because he cannot turn from the dictates of his heart?"

"I shouldn't think so. Virtue, old boy, is not as golden as it has been painted. A girl who has lived is no worse than one who has lost a husband through law or mishap."

Fang nodded. "You speak like a Chinese. You seek to inject reason into emotion." He stopped and looked up. "Was that something—" But Rayne had already pounced on the little white object.

He unwrapped a piece of tattered paper from a pebble and managed to read the slanted backhand writing. "Hope." The one word. Nothing else.

"Woman's writing," said Rayne.

"How do you know?"

"See that slant? I never saw a man write like that."

"But what woman?"

"There you have me. It would only have been one of them who has the run of the place. Marlene or Van der Vanter's daughter, but I didn't see her."

Fang Gat returned to his seat. "In any event, it would appear that we have allies. I have a human breast and in it I can feel hope springing eternally."

Food came as the dungeon darkened because of a rain squall and falling twilight and they could not see who lowered it. They could see his silhouette against the sky, but there was insufficient light for identification.

"Hello, up there!" called Rayne.

"Untie rope." And that was all. They untied the rope and found a small tin pail filled with stink fish cooked in cocoanut oil and rice, mixed with several herbs and vegetables. It was not palatable, but more in quantity than they had expected. There was a huge breadfruit that had been roasted in an open fire and though Rayne did not care for the dry tasteless viand, he ate it, nevertheless, in place of the fish, feeling that he should keep up his strength no matter how gloomy the future seemed.

"Open the door." The voice seemed to come from so close that Rayne looked at Fang Gat.

"Did you say something?"

"No. Some of these old ruins have amazing acoustics. The door!"

Rayne turned and saw a stream of flickering light pour through as the massive door swung noiselessly open. They could see a woman come through, then the door closed behind her and save for the small torch she carried, all was darkness again. It was Marlene and she walked toward them, having regained her disturbingly sinuous walk and heavy-lidded seductiveness. She walked over to them and stood for a moment, looking into Fang Gat's immobile face.

"I had to come," she said in a soft rich contralto.

"Why?" he asked flatly.

"Because—Fang, I used to love you. You once loved me. Isn't that reason enough?"

He nodded slowly. "I suppose it is. I, however, would have preferred to think of you as I once knew you when you were fresh and unspoiled. And clean."

"Then you think I'm dirty?"

"Not really. Not in the sense you think. You've distributed your body, of course, to Moak and others probably, but that you would be associated with him, knowing him to be a pirate, a criminal and a murderer is another matter. Again, why?"

Her eyes filled with tears. "I wanted money, Fang. I want lots and lots of it. Enough so that I can do just as I please, whenever I please. I never realized what a liberator money was until my family was so unreasonable about you. I was their prisoner, forced to do their bidding because I was economically dependent on them. I was in the employ of the Red Cross for a time, then I had a chance to take this position with the UN. I met Moak and he told me about Van der Vanter who was an old man, with a fortune in diamonds and gold. He had a fortune, but no diamonds or gold. I married him."

"And Moak killed him." Fang was standing, his eyes greenish in the flickering light.

Her shoulders slumped. "If he did, then he was very clever about it. The doctor said that it was just a heart condition, something he had had a long time. I don't say Moak didn't do it."

"That is very sporting of you, I'm sure."

She looked at him for some time, her lips trembling a little, her eyes deep pools of mystic light. "Fang, I don't think you even like me any more."

"Should I?"

She made a hopeless little motion with her shoulders and looked at Rayne. "Taneeta said to tell you that she's all right."

"Is she?"

"I think so. Kong Ghee is watching her."

"Who is he?"

"Half Malay and half Chinese. He is also after the box."

"What do you know of the box?" asked Rayne, coming to his feet with a bound.

"Moak has it. I don't know where. He expects to get a fortune for it. I'm financing him and he'll split with me."

Fang Gat's laugh was harsh and insulting. "I suppose it would be too much to expect you to be lovely and intelligent as well."

She flushed ruddily. "What do you mean by that crack?—that is, other than its being a dirty crack?"

"Didn't Moak tell you how he got the box?"

"He bought it."

"He killed the man who wanted to sell it. The price was too high. He would have killed Granger as soon as he got back here with the schooner. He said so."

Her eyes held his for a moment, then they crossed to Rayne's. "Is he telling the truth?"

Rayne shrugged. "You know him better than you do me. You should know what to believe."

She sighed and the firm globes of her lush breasts moved inside the cloth of her sarong. "I don't know ..."

"Then I'll tell you," said Fang Gat harshly. "Once he gets the money, he'll do one of two things. He'll disappear or he'll kill you. It makes little difference which. He can buy many women like you—maybe not on credit, but then he won't have to."

She winced at his words. "You can be cruel."

"I have been many things," said Fang Gat coolly. "In California, I was a fool."

"Why do you say that?" She seemed a little breathless for some reason.

"Because in the only country where such a thing can safely be combated, I allowed parental interference to stand in my way. I should have married you then, even if it couldn't have lasted."

"Why couldn't it?" Her voice was almost a whisper.

A sneer curled his lips. "Because it is fated that I serve, not grow rich. You couldn't have stood it."

She was silent for a moment, twisting the torch in her hands as it grew short and hot. Her eyes found his again. "It was because of you that I grew to hate the things I had to do because I was not financially free." She turned and walked away, the torch guttering out before she reached the door. They heard her call out, saw the light of the torch from the other side. Then there was darkness.

"And all the time the idea never occurred to us to make a break for it as she went out," raged Rayne, bitterly.

Fang Gat lifted his shoulders. "Is it important? Is anything important?"

Rayne stretched out on his end of the stone slab and thought for a long time. "It seems you were right about the old Malay servant."

"That was Oldwick. I don't see how the old man ever hopes to accomplish anything by himself. He might stick around until some opportunity presents itself. I wonder how Marlene discovered that he, too, was after the box. And what did she mean about Kong Ghee watching Taneeta?"

Rayne's body grew suddenly cold. "I don't know. What would Moak care about a one-eyed old man if he wanted Taneeta?"

"I think," said the other, "that Marlene is more of a deterrent to him that Kong Ghee would be. Maybe she meant she left him to watch while she was down here."

Rayne inexplicably felt instantly better, but Fang soon fixed that.

"I think you should brace yourself for the worst," he said. "Suppose it does happen? It won't kill her and in a few months she will forget about it."

"Sometimes I could choke you," snarled Rayne, sitting up and sweating with exasperation. "We are down here, and as far as I can see, are likely to stay."

"The Mohammedans have a word for it."

"And that is?"

"*Kismet.*"

Dawn lighted the square above them, midday made it as bright as turquoise and twilight turned it the color of aquamarine and so the days passed. Rayne had grown sullen and uncommunicative, walking restlessly around the walls thinking, searching for some chink in that impregnable fortress of incarceration; while Fang Gat, phlegmatic and unemotional on the surface, at least sat calmly, his face inscrutable, and waited.

Rayne, returning from one of his interminable tours of inspection, stood before his friend and said, "Say something."

Fang Gat smiled. "I'm sorry. I can no more help being what I am than you can help being what you are. We both await fate in our own way."

Rayne flopped on the bench dispiritedly and said, "Sorry. I guess I'm tottering near where Perc was last week. Fish and rice and breadfruit, dampness, plain water, and no way out of this grave or I'd have found it. Every time I think of Marlene going out of that door as casually as Moak came in and me sitting here on my dead can doing nothing about it—I deserve to stay here."

"And what would you have done had you gotten out?"

"Gotten shot, probably. But at least it would have been doing something."

"And all to no end. That Occidental drive to hurry, even to death—" He cut it off. "Must be chow time."

It was, and the basket turned slowly as it came down through the dark hole. Rayne walked over to it, disengaged the rope and gave it the usual tug to signal it free. Then his hand touched something strange. It was a piece of cold machined metal that gave him a thrill, a jagged icy shock that danced through his senses. He must have made some sound trying to choke back a yell of delight because Fang Gat came over to him.

"What is it?"

"A good old Tommy," hissed Rayne, crazily. "M 1928 with two grips and an L drum. Boy, oh boy. Can you make a light?"

"I can, but let's make it out of sight of the opening. Someone might be watching." Fang Gat extracted a small pile of papers from his wallet and touched the edge of one of them with his lighter which he had been using sparingly. In the dim yellow light, they could see the wicked lines of the submachine gun, four cartons of service ammunition and an extra drum.

"Let's load them now," said Rayne, excitedly.

"I'm afraid you'll have to do it. I've only used the straight clip type—thirty rounds."

Rayne cackled aloud. "I'll do it and love it. Break open those cartons and feed them to me as I ask for them. Never mind the light. I can do this blindfolded. Even has a Cutts Compensator. Wonder where he got this weapon?"

"Who?"

Rayne blinked. "Damned if I know. Do you suppose Marlene is still carrying the torch for you?"

Fang Gat grunted. "I have no money."

"Let's not be stupid about that," said Rayne with somber intensity. "What I hear now is *face* talking."

"Maybe. I guess you're right." Fang sighed.

"Better let the heart take over again, son. Face can be awfully expensive at times, you know."

Fang subsided and listened to the metallic sounds as Rayne happily fed the drum to the limit with the stubby deadly cartridges. He wound the key, counting the clicks, and then there was a louder click and the sound of the bolt being snapped home. "Now!"

Fang Gat recoiled involuntarily. Accustomed to violence and sudden death, he nevertheless was not prepared for one word so impregnated with cold murderous anticipation.

"Just let me get my head above that damn square hole," continued the voice, as hard as razor steel. "Let's keep all this debris, Fang, so it won't show if anyone comes in."

On an impulse, the Chinese had struck his lighter into activity and looked full into Rayne's face. It was white and cut with taut lines, shining brightly with sweat.

Fang laughed softly. "You're afraid."

There was a short silence and when he spoke Rayne's throat seemed to have tightened. "All right. So you know."

"I know. I also know that even a cobra is more deadly when afraid. Right now, Rayne, you're the most dangerous man on this island. Even in this dungeon."

Rayne said nothing, but went to the bench and sat. Did you hang onto everything that came down? Those cartons, I mean. They might have a message. In fact, I think we ought to examine them now."

"Very well. Let's light the paper gain. I snuffed it out."

Fang Gat lit the little pile of seared paper again and Rayne turned the boxes over swiftly. Then his breath hissed audibly. "Here it is. 'When the basket comes down empty, the rope will be secured topside.' "

Fang Gat put his foot on the flame and again they were in total darkness. They walked back to the bench and sat down, tearing all the cartons into bits and dividing them among their pockets. Then they gathered stone chips and debris, hiding the weapon well.

"How good are you at climbing ropes?" asked Fang.

"I don't know," admitted Rayne. "I could, I guess. We've climbed them in training."

"Yes, but you climbed them and then came down. This will be different. For two feet the rope will be tight against the rock."

"Yeah. I hadn't thought of that."

"And you'll be carrying the gun."

"That's right."

"So I'll go up first. I was a fair pole vaulter at the university. I'll climb as far as I can, then put my feet up and vault the rest of the way. Then, when you come up, I can give you a hand."

Silence fell between them and in the dungeon it was a silence that they had never experienced before. It seemed to cling to them like a wet black vapor that had choking qualities. Not a single sound of any sort came to their ears, save their own heart-beats which were plainly audible.

They slept, finally, and day broke above the square of light. It brightened and faded toward evening from twilight again and the awful silence seemed to tear at their nerves. There were sup-posed to be rats and Rayne would have almost welcomed them as a diversion—anything to blot out that aching pall of velvety nothingness that made their ears ring with soundless shrieks and every motion of their limbs sound like branches breaking.

Fang Gat had an old shoulder wound that Rayne had come to recognize from the agonized scraping of the bones as plainly as though amplified electrically. He said it didn't bother him any more, but to his friend it was like a child's fingernails drawn slowly across a blackboard. So Rayne began his pacing of the walls, even though it was too dark to see, and when the basket came down with food, it was all he could do to keep from screaming because it had not been empty.

CHAPTER NINE

AFTER THEY HAD eaten, a light appeared at the square and they could see the grinning figure of Moak standing triumphant and unconquerable at the lip of the opening. His right hand held a torch of plaited cocoanut leaves and in his left was a shapeless figure.

With a heave, he hurled the figure toward Rayne and called, "Catch."

Rayne, shaken in a split second by the knowledge that the figure was human, lunged forward and made an attempt to break the fall of the body. It struck him and stretched his tendons to the point of bursting. His vertabrae cracked alarmingly and his arm muscles went dead as he pitched forward on the body he had attempted to catch. He got up dizzily and looked at Moak who was laughing uproariously.

"Good try, Rayne. Maybe she hasn't anything but a broken back. Might live for days like that." With a shake of the torch that sent sparks spinning crazily downward, he walked away and left them in darkness.

"Strike a light," said Rayne, frantically, and when the feeble glow reached the girl's face, he almost fainted with relief. It was not Taneeta. "Who is it?" The voice was a harsh croak.

"I'm not acquainted with the lady," said Fang Gat easily as he examined her. "I may add that your heroism was not for nothing. All I can find is a nasty cut from a blow that her heavy hair turned more than a little. The blood is dried a little, so she didn't even get that in the fall." Fang drew away with a hiss and a Chinese curse that made Rayne blink. *"Ill begotten son of all and father of none."* The feeble light flickered out and Fang sank back to the bench, his face wet with the sweat of horror.

His long fingers cracked loudly in the gloom as he wrenched at his hands in an excess of futile rage. "May the site of every hair on his foul body be the repository of a thousand boils ..."

"What's the matter with you?" yelled Rayne, his nerves leaping out of control.

Fang changed to English. "Did you not see her feet?"

"No."

"A torture commonly ascribed to the Chinese. Her toes are great raw blisters. A sharp sliver of bamboo is inserted beneath the nails and then set afire ..." He broke into Chinese again. "For this there could be but one death. And it insufficient. My friend, I beg of you—ask anything you will, but give this man to me should we ever get out of this alive. I hope there are ants on the island."

Rayne shuddered, but struck one of his own precious hoard of matches. He got up and went to sit by Fang. "I'll not only give him to you—I'll watch. That must be Van der Vanter's daughter."

Fang wiped his wet face with a trembling hand. "Wanton cruelty, cruelty for personal gain." He choked up and was silent for a while. "I wonder what she knew that was important to him?"

"Let's revive her. We have water in a container."

"No. Let's not revive her until we have done something about her feet. There should be plenty of cocoanut oil in the bucket. I'll tear up my shirt. Fetch one of those ancient stone containers. What oil we don't use on her, we will use for a light. I should have thought of it before." In the smelly, flickering light, they bound the girl's feet with cloth soaked in stinking fishy cocoanut oil, the very smell of the charred flesh making Rayne grind his teeth against repeated waves of nausea.

"Lord, if our friend will just send down the empty basket," he prayed.

"The note, as you said, was in a woman's hand writing. Suppose it is her? We're lost if that is true."

"I won't believe it. I can't. The note said 'Hope' and that's what I'm going to do."

He examined the slight figure of the girl wrapped in batik. The wrap had come loose and exposed one smooth flank of shimmering ivory skin and a single breast. It was a body that, in spite of small size—she would stand only a little over five feet—had been carved with exquisite care; her breast as firm as a mango, shaped like a fragile teacup, sharp-pointed and so smoothly surfaced that Rayne swallowed involuntarily and covered it, flushing as Fang laughed softly.

"I revere them, too, but I do not share your Victorian shame of nudity."

"It wasn't that, exactly. It was like peeking where we had no business."

"She is our business exclusively."

"What is she?"

"Half Dutch—if she's Van der Vanter's daughter. There is some Chinese and possibly Malay. She is very beautiful."

Rayne stood up and let Fang add the finishing touches. "And that son of a bitch that chunked her down here like a sack of chicken guts ..."

"He's mine. You have promised."

"I'll give him to you alive. That's all I promise."

"That is enough, but I want him sufficiently alive for my purpose."

The girl gave a whimpering sigh and opened her eyes. They widened with horror and she screamed, a tearing horrid leap of sound that seemed to stretch every muscle of her throat. Rayne clapped a hand over her mouth and felt the steel of her marvelous muscles ripple with effort, although she did not try to sit up.

"Easy, baby," he soothed. "You're with friends. We've tried to bind your feet, so don't pitch around or you'll ruin our efforts."

She relaxed a little and sobs started from her throat. They grew faster and faster until at last she was writhing and screaming again. Rayne slapped her hard, then lifted her to a sitting position and held her close, letting her cry her nerves into a state of peace.

"It is an amazing thing the power Western men have over women all over the world," soliloquized Fang Gat, marveling at Rayne's handling of the girl whose weeping had almost ceased. She still clutched him with a hard, starved frenzy, as though to let him go would drop her back into the pit of horror which she could recall too well.

When finally she could talk, she cuddled close to Rayne, still afraid to get very far from the pillar of strength he had provided.

"Why did he do that to you?" asked Fang Gat.

Her English was quaint and delightful. "Because I saw where he hid the box. I took it and hid it myself."

"Did he make you tell?"

She nodded, fresh tears coming from her eyes. Her face was that of a beautiful child's, oval with features very regular and piquant. Her eyes were tremendous and green, shadowed by sweeping black lashes, and her brows were thick and unplucked. She smiled tremulously. "He had a bad time making me tell, though, and I told Kong Ghee. When he hides it again, Kong Ghee will watch him."

"Do your feet hurt?" asked Rayne, solicitously. She nodded and her eyes filled with tears again.

"They hurt terribly, but not as much as they did." She sighed and leaned her head against his shoulder. "You are very kind," she said, softly.

"That is it," averred Fang Gat. "The Western mind is always filled with compassion and women of any land like that very much."

"Only my father was ever kind to me," said the girl, wistfully. "And Mr. Oldwick."

The two men exchanged quick glances. "Perc?" Rayne put the question. "What did he do?"

"He didn't do anything. He only treated me as though I were a human and not a bitch of an animal."

"Well," breathed Fang Gat. "Mr. Oldwick is not so crazy that he has lost his rearing."

"He's not crazy at all," she defended stoutly. "You'll see."

Rayne sighed and stroked her fine hair that was heavy and midnight black. He had little faith in Perc's ability to do anything with the freedom he enjoyed.

The door of the dungeon opened and a blade of light showed Marlene coming in. Behind her were three heavily armed Malays who effectually aborted Rayne's sudden leap of hope.

Fang Gat rose to his feet. "What do you want?"

"Someone said he threw Loa into the dungeon."

"He did. Mr. Cantey providentially broke her fall at some risk to his own neck." Fang Gat stopped, looked queerly at Marlene, then continued. "In view of the fact that he practically burned off her toes, throwing her down here wasn't as cruel as it might seem."

Marlene turned chalk white and put her fingers to her temples, uttering a despairing little sound.

"Very dramatic," commented Fang Gat, sarcastically. "Would you like to go now? Or will you be kicked out?"

Still watching the bandaged toes of the girl, she backed away a few steps, then turned and stumbled toward the door. It closed behind her and there was a long silence.

"Sometimes," said Loa, "I like her. And at others, I don't. She has kept him from taking me against my will. Some man will take me one day, but I prefer to want him with all my heart so that the wonder of him shall choke me and drench me with a heavenly joy and I shall scream and hold him close throughout the whole night. And when he has tasted of my kisses and when I have given him the wonder of my body, the warmth and depth of it, the taste and feel of my breasts, he will not desire the next woman he sees as that beast does, but will want to return to another night such as I shall have made for him in the beginning."

Rayne, swept into the peculiar poetry of her vision, drawn by the smooth music of her voice, leaned forward, wanting to hear more, but Fang Gat interposed.

"How old are you, my child?"

"I will be sixteen in a few weeks. I am very old, but my father would let me have none of men."

They exchanged glances and Rayne felt a little disembodied, listening to a fifteen-year-old draw such mental pictures.

"My father is dead now," she said, "and soon I shall have a man of my choosing."

"Suppose," said Rayne, "this man does not love you?"

"How will he help it?" she asked candidly, pulling aside her sarong and showing a leg as smooth as marble and golden in the yellow light. "Am I not beautiful? Am I not desirable?"

"There can be but one answer to that, little flower," said Fang Gat, kindly. "He will not be able to resist you."

"You see," she said smugly to Rayne. "And I must choose soon or I shall be too old to be lovely."

"I think at the age of forty you will be even more lovely than you are at present."

Her dark somber eyes sought his. "I think you are a very kind man. If Taneeta had not already claimed you, I should choose you for myself."

Rayne felt his face grow hot and the sound of Fang Gat's laugh did not help.

There was little sleep for them that night because the girl moaned while asleep and tossed and moved about when awake. Rayne wondered how she could even catch a nap with her feet so horribly mutilated.

In the light of the morning, he could better appreciate the girl's confidence in holding her man; she was a classic miniature in gold, bronze and ivory. She sat up and tossed her hair several times, letting it fall back to its severe shoulder length bob, looked at her dirty hands and nails and made a distasteful face.

"When," she asked Rayne, "are we going to escape?"

He laughed shortly. "That's what I'd like to know. Maybe you can be as patient as Fang Gat who has no nerves in his body. As for me, I'm having to hold on to keep from screaming."

She shrugged. "I can be patient, but I don't like it. I want a bath and some clean clothes."

"We have no facilities for that here," Fang Gat assured her.

"But I want to—" She stopped and looked appealingly at Rayne but she was not embarrassed.

"Go to the far end of the dungeon, Loa," he said gently. "We will keep our heads averted."

She shrugged. "It wasn't that so much. I like you and your friend and I wouldn't mind, only … it doesn't seem a very nice thing to do."

"It is not to be helped," put in Fang Gat. "I hope we will not be here for long."

She stood up and promptly fell to her knees. "I can't walk," she sobbed.

"Hell," ejaculated Rayne. "I should have known that." He picked her up easily and carried her fifty feet away where a stone pillar some six feet in diameter offered privacy.

He sat her gently down and said, "Call me, Loa, when you're ready."

Her eyes were spaniel soft. "You don't have to leave. Just turn your back." He walked around the pillar and waited till she called him, then he picked her up and brought her back to the bench where Fang Gat sat.

That day passed faster than had the others as Loa's store of small talk and frank personal opinions and imaginings seemed without end. Her spirit hadn't been damped by the torture and she was a delight to them, talking with naive freedom, weighing them both and rejecting them as possible husbands and giving her reasons freely. Rayne was already spoken for by Taneeta and to Loa this was an insuperable obstacle. Fang Gat was a soldier who would never be home to see his children born—if, indeed, he would be there to father them in the first place.

It was dark now, and Loa was dozing with her head in Rayne's lap. If her feet hurt, she refused to admit it, declaring their treatment nothing short of magic and that in a matter of hours she would be afoot again and ready to fight by their sides when rescue should come. She never wavered in her conviction that in some manner they would be saved.

The silence had descended again and in the gloom of the cavern it seemed thick enough to feel and taste. Of a sudden, it was rent by the razor rip of a Schmeisser fired on full automatic. There was a scream and a patter above of running feet. Again the machine pistol vomited out a burst of bullets and again came the scream, this time right over their heads. There was the sound of a falling body and a tinny scrape as something slid over the stone floor; then it fell with a dull clink, almost at their feet. And again silence filled the cavern.

Like a cat, Fang Gat pounced upon it, although Rayne could not see how he accomplished it in the darkness.

"Quick," hissed the former, "lift the stone bench if you can."

Rayne strained until his ears rang and blood rushed noisily to his head, but he couldn't budge the slab. "Can't move it," he panted.

Fang Gat dropped to his knees by the girl. "Take this, little flower, and when we lift the stone, place it carefully beneath the slab and the support. Understand?"

"Yes."

Combining efforts, Fang Gat and Rayne strove mightily and just managed to lift the slab enough that Loa could slip the object under it.

"You can let it down now," she said calmly.

They were sweating and winded when she gave the word and hardly had they seated themselves when a light appeared at the opening with Moak's convulsed face behind it.

"Did a box fall down there?" he asked foolishly.

"What sort of box," asked Rayne, "and what's going on up there, a massacre?"

"Which you may join any moment," he snarled back. He waved an imperious arm to his men. "It must have fallen down there and since they can't hide it, we'll look."

Ten minutes later, a baffled Moak stood back and surveyed his prisoners through slitted lids. "There is only one thing that saves you from just such a dose as this girl got," he said malignantly. "Kong Ghee may have had help and maybe the help made off with it. It's jolly well impossible to hide anything down here and I've searched you thoroughly, so I know it isn't here. Be glad that I'm a civilized man, else I'd burn your feet just for the fun of it."

Loa whimpered from where he had thrown her when he searched her; she was naked, since he had ripped the sarong from her body.

"What are you chirping about?" he snarled, his face twisted and sweaty. "Looks to me like you'd be chipper at not having a broken neck when I threw you down here and Sir Galahad caught you. Ah!" He turned around and beckoned to a burly brown man who appeared to be the leader or sergeant of his men. "Tical, you have long wanted this woman, have you not?"

The man grinned, showing his betel-stained teeth. "*Tuan,* there is no woman in the world I would rather possess."

"Then take her. Hey—you men out in the corridor! Come in and watch the fun. Tical may need help, too."

Rayne drew tighter and tighter, his eyes cold and dead in his head. Muscles tightened across his back until it was as hard as teak. His fingers crooked like talons and though Fang Gat spoke soft words of caution in his ears, he couldn't hear a thing but the hateful voice of Moak urging the grinning man toward Loa who, now thoroughly frightened, drew away as the man approached. She looked at Rayne and her child's chin trembled and her great eyes held mute entreaty.

"Stop him, Moak!" said Rayne in such a terrible voice that Tical stopped, his eyes slated with fear for a moment.

Moak's laugh came harsh and loud. "Take her," he ordered. "And make it good. Think, man, all your friends are watching and I also."

Tical reassured, squatted beside the naked girl and unwound his breech cloth, laying his *kris* carefully aside. "You are lucky," he told her cajolingly, "to have a man like me steal your virginity." He fell forward suddenly, enveloping her helplessly in his arms. In a flash, she was hopelessly vulnerable and with a little cry, fell back and gave up.

The tightening procees that Rayne had undergone could no longer be endured. With a cry more animal than human, he made a sweeping motion and from the carefully camouflaged scattering of debris beneath the bench, he came up with the sub-machine gun. His face was white and set in a horrible grin as he brought the muzzle around in a blaze of fire and whistling slugs. The first burst tore the Schmeisser from Moak's grasp and the man behind him lunged forward with three bullets through the chest.

Again the muzzle swung in a short arc, still vomiting slugs and flame into the packed mass of men. He held the trigger down in defiance of good gunmanship and swung the muzzle back and forth like a hose of death. The muzzle flame lit up his face and the terrible grin flashed as red as the flame.

With a leap, Fang Gat cleared the prostrate form of Moak, seized Tical's *kris*, and split the man's skull with one terrific sweep of the heavy blade. On the floor a man was crawling toward the Schmeisser on one hand and his knees, the other arm hanging in threads. Upon him Fang turned the *kris* with one full-armed stroke that girded off the bone of the head and took away half his face.

The submachine gun went silent and the effect was almost a physical blow. The dungeon was smoky with the fumes of cordite and on the floor lay the ten men whom Moak had brought with him.

One attempted to rise with a carbine in his hand and the sub-gun stuttered out three rounds and he sank back.

Above a torch flickered and Rayne looked up to see Perc signaling frantically. "The rope, you chaps, it's all secure." An ear-shocking burst ripped from Rayne's gun and a man fell headlong into the dungeon, his *kris* having missed Perc by inches. Looking quickly back, Perc used the rope himself and slid down to join them.

"Rum. Several more coming. Thanks. Sorry and all that. Hated to bung away, but no arms, you know. Jolly well can use this trinket." He grabbed the Schmeisser from the floor and the arriving men were caught full in the face by combined fire from Rayne and Perc. They fell away and then silence settled again.

Perc leaped to aid Loa and fumbled futilely, trying to help her arrange the batik becomingly.

Fang Gat sat upon the bench and looked interestedly at the *kris* that still dripped red.

Rayne, still holding the Thompson close to his body, sank to the floor, trembling with reaction.

"What say we bung the hell out of here?" put in Perc. "I see the door is open."

CHAPTER TEN

THE SUN SHONE brightly as they sat in the early morning shade of the verandah-like front of the frowning building that fronted the water. They ate mangos and papayas and young cocoanuts. Then came toasted breadfruit and eggs of some shore bird that the *Lena*'s steward had found.

Marlene sat a little aloof and said nothing as she ate, while Loa and Perc scattered inanities at each other so thickly that Rayne, in spite of his euphoria was annoyed.

"Restrain your understandable irritation," said Fang Gat, smiling. "They are both young and neither of us is."

"Yes," put in Taneeta, "there'll be many years between my own foolishness and the education you must give me."

"What about Moak?" asked Rayne.

"Moak was not badly done in, I'm glad to say." Fang Gat's eyes smouldered as he spoke. "And there are a very vicious species of ants on the island."

"Oh, no," said Taneeta, aghast.

"Please, let me add my voice to that plea," said Marlene, coming over to them.

"Your plea sounds strangely enough," said Fang Gat, "especially since you have seen Loa's feet."

"As for Taneeta," said Rayne harshly with his first show of authority, "she will remain silent."

"As for Marlene," said Fang Gat with deceptive gentleness, "she will also remain silent. If you wish, my dear, you may have Moak when the ants are done with him."

She bit her lip. "I think you're inhuman." It sounded empty—apparently to Marlene as well as the others, because she flushed.

"Your humane concern is sudden," Fang Gat reminded her. "Where was it when a million dollars was at stake?"

Her eyes filled with tears and she walked away to sit slumped against a stone column.

After breakfast they dawdled around as though reluctant to leave the new atmosphere of total freedom; besides, the place was undeniably beautiful. Finally Fang Gat called Koa, Tanala and the other Kanakas. They had all been placed in another prison and had been released not long previously. Gorged with food, they were now in high spirits.

"Go into *pui-pui* and bring along me man Moak," he said to them. "He gottem pain, but he not bad, so you need not be too careful, b'long him."

They grinned, bobbed their heads and departed at a trot.

Rayne and Fang Gat went with them to the head of the steps leading down to the dungeon and there they waited until the men appeared, carrying Moak between them. His old grin had not left him.

"What ho? It seems that there has been some table turning."

"That's only a part, my friend," said Fang Gat gently. "You will now taste some of what you fed Loa—only there will be no one to call off the ants."

Moak's face went ashen and he turned to Rayne. "You're a white man. You can't let him do it. Not to me, a member of your own race. Cantey, tell him he can't do it. Tell him!"

Rayne's hand flashed and hard knuckles cracked across Moak's mouth. "All I want to hear from you is your last breath. Bring him along, boys."

They carried him down the main thoroughfare of the city, flanked by buildings of white stone, weathered and streaked with lichen and moss, but still stout and unbroken, except where stubborn trees had taken root and split the blocks of stone.

They came to the edge of the jungle after a twenty-minute walk and old Koa, with a nose like a hound, found what they wanted—a four-foot high mound that straggled upward in ragged ascent. With a swift kick, he sent it tumbling, while Tanala drove four stout stakes into the ground. A mass of infuriated ants rustled out, seething in red masses, dashing about, searching for the wrecker of their home. Moak's eyes bulged as he watched them. Knots of muscle stood out on the sides of his jaw and sweat ran in rivulets from his face.

"I suppose any plea would be of no use," he said hoarsely, "so have at your barbaric play."

"What would you call what you did to Loa?" asked Rayne tightly.

Moak shrugged. "I've been no angel. Don't get the idea I'm begging."

They picked him up and spread-eagled him over the ant hill, tying his feet to the stakes expertly, and in a flash the red, maddened horde poured over his naked body like a breath of acid fire. Muscles stood out on his limbs like cords and his teeth shone dryly in a supreme muscular spasm; then, Fang Gat solemnly drew his recovered Mauser and shot him neatly between the eyes.

"It behooves civilized man to remain in possession of some of his acquired qualities," he said quietly. "Not even to Moak, could I become Moak."

Rayne dashed the sweat from his eyes and swallowed with relief. "And you cease being a mere man, Fang Gat. You are a prince among men. I respect you greatly for that act."

"I appreciate your respect. But I acted as I did for the sake of my own, which after all is even more important to me."

The Kanakas, manifestly disappointed at being cheated of their sport, fell in behind the two men as they turned away from what little remained of Stanley Moak, soldier of fortune.

The *Lena* rode the waves toward the setting sun blithely, and even the disturbed flying fishes seemed to be fleeing in sport rather than in fear. Perc, who had not been able to get very far away from Loa for some time, approached Rayne where the latter was talking to old Koa.

"You savvy course b'long Macao?"

Koa shrugged. "Long time savvy course. Mebbyso not navigator—many time hold wheel on course."

"You savvy reefs and shoals b'long course?"

"Me savvy."

"Then you take her in. When we make port, I sell the *Lena*. Divide with crew."

Koa demurred. "My word! You not fella marster nenny more?"

"No more," said Rayne firmly. "Alla same finish this time."

Koa nodded slowly, then turned away only to turn back again. "You buying schooner, Koa being number one boy nenny time. My word!"

Rayne grinned and nodded. "Any time I buying schooner I am sending for Koa—chop-chop."

"More better you hurry, chop-chop. Koa making old." He walked away, shaking his head.

"I say ..." Perc put in hastily, having shuffled about, waiting for the conversation to end.

"What is it, Perc?"

Perc wiped his forehead and shuffled his feet again. "Fearfully embarrassin' and all that, dear ole person, but I have a problem. In a manner of speakin'. That is, we—" He broke off suddenly and swallowed rather uneasily.

"You mean you and Loa have a problem, don't you?" Rayne could hardly keep back a laugh.

"Er ... right ho," he squeaked, reddening. "Not bein' done, y'know. Matter of East and West and never the twain and all that sort of Kipling puff. Not being a *sahib*—if you know what I mean."

"I think I know what you mean. But what's your problem? If you've made up your mind to be a *pukka sahib,* then where is the problem?"

Perc squirmed in torment. "Never been one of these shockin' ole rugged charactered johnnies and I find that no matter what my head tells me, the ole ticker doesn't seem impressed and there you are. Or rather, there I am. Matter of fact, where the ruddy hell am I?" Perc mopped his face in trembling anguish.

"I'm sure I don't know where the ruddy hell you are, Perc, but I do know this. Kipling has been dead a long time and I doubt this *pukka sahib* business was ever what it was cracked up to be, in truth. Seems like the old chutney-flavored colonels married wispy fragile things more to adorn their homes than their beds. This isn't the day of Balaklava and the British square and Kitchener and Gordon and the rest of the convoluted Victorian era, however honored it once was. When you come to realize that, then I think a lot of your troubles will clarify themselves and even end."

Perc's eyes misted over. "Dashed kind of you to talk to me this way, takin' into mind all you've done before. Have the impulse to fall at your dear ole feet, or some other embarrassingly humble act. Always needed talkin' to like that. Can't live in the past forever. Not by a shot, you can't. What's wrong with the lovely creature, after all?"

Rayne's smile was kindly. "I saw quite a lot of her. When her toes heal, there won't be a flaw on her. She's the East and you'll have to understand her and be tolerant until she learns your ways and the ways of the world. In a way I guess it's too bad she has to learn that."

"Right ho." Perc straightened up and grinned from ear to ear. "Crushin' lot of weight off my chest. Feel like a new man. Have to watch her, though. Her sense of morality isn't what it could be." He turned with a light step and walked away whistling.

The next morning Loa came up to Rayne as he stepped from his cabin. "May I speak with you a moment, sir?"

"Sure. Let's walk toward the bow."

She wore a pair of Taneeta's white shorts that were too large for her and a twist of yellow silk over her small breasts. She was adorably comical, but her face was serious.

"Didn't I tell you?"

"Er—what?"

"I told you."

"You told me what, Loa?"

"That once giving the wonder that is me to the wonder that is my man, he'd never escape me."

"Yes," he nodded, "you told me."

Her face changed subtly. It smoothed out and a look of deep glutted satisfaction came over it, lending it an aura of almost super-human confidence. Rayne tingled as the implication of what she was saying came to him.

"Last night?" he suggested tentatively.

She nodded and a slow smile drew her lips back from her perfect white teeth. "Last night... in the dinghy. I did it. He tried to resist, as I knew he would, but he couldn't. Heaven is not a place where one goes after death. It is a state one reaches in the warm bath of love, here in life. He will remember last night and many nights to come and he will never be able to think of another woman for I shall fill his life so full of love that even in his dreams there will always be me and the love I can give in so many ways. I can be soft and clinging like a young puppy, or I can be fierce and bruising like a tiger. I can hurt him where ecstasy loves hurt, or I can soothe him when life has bruised him. I can draw him out of himself and out of the pain of all his past and I can show him a future that is filled to the brim with new and more beautiful love than he in his sort of life could possibly know." She looked at Rayne, her eyes sparkling and clear as gems. She clapped her small hands ecstatically. "He is a very simple man, really. Young and so stupid. I shall teach him what I wish that he knows. I shall bend him to my will and it will not hurt because at the end of it all there will be my love; and, to him, my love shall be as the peak of a mountain in the tender morning sun, shining always for him to see and comfort him in the knowledge that it is his—for all time."

Rayne gazed at her golden little body in stupefaction, at her face so transported in the utter surety of her convictions, exalted in the fires of a love; she made him feel a sort of stumbling neophyte, small before the inferno contained in her tiny body.

Finally, he found his voice. "I shall love you always, Loa, and I shall think of you as someone who could draw not only her lover from his fears and shyness, but also anyone whom you honored with your friendship. In Perc you have a good man. I feel that you will make him good. In you he has the world. If he has you, he needs nothing else."

She gurgled delightedly and, bending forward, kissed his hand, making him squirm inwardly. "I knew you'd say something nice to me. That's why I told you. I haven't told anyone else. I can tell when someone is my friend for the best and the worst. I'm not ashamed of what I did and I shall do it again and again because I love him. I have no doubt that the time will come when he can think only of his love for me." She turned and walked away, her smooth shapely little hips swaying with a native grace that white women can only affect—and when they do, that motion of loveliness becomes one of lewdness.

Rayne stood in the bow for some time, letting the breezes play under his thin shirt. It had not grown overly hot as yet and he was still savoring the effect of Loa's conversation. Their mission was nearly complete and had been more successfully achieved than he had thought possible. Seeing Fang Gat come from the chart room, he called to him.

"Isn't the secret of the box nagging at you?"

Fang shook his head. "Not as yet. I had thought—subject to your own opinion—that I should like to open it before my father. He is an old man and his days are not too many. It would afford him great pleasure. I don't think there will be any disagreement as to our goal once it is opened."

"That suits me. I wasn't too sure at first that we would agree, Fang. Now I'm as certain as you are. I have learned a lot in the last month."

"And who among us hasn't? Witness the hapless Perc, who smuggled us the submachine gun and was ready to risk his life to see that we got out of the dungeon. And I dare say Marlene has learned a lesson also."

"What about Loa?"

Fang Gat laughed. "That one? She has been so busy teaching, she has had very little time to learn."

"That one," amended Rayne with flat conviction, "already knows everything. She doesn't need to learn."

"The gods have been good," intoned Fang So, solemnly. "I greet you, Mr. Cantey, with the same emotion with which I greet my own son. While you waited he has told me of your venture." The old man motioned to a small yellow man in the clothes of a workman. "You may ply thy devil iron and open the box."

The electric soldering iron soon melted the box into two halves. Then Fang So spoke to the workman again. "Now you will take your iron and depart. Your work is done. Mr. Cantey, to you will go the privilege of opening the packet."

It was an oilskin packet sealed with wax and in point of size not very impressive. Rayne broke the seals and opened it, spreading the contents out on a small low table. Breaths hissed as they leaned forward to look.

Fang Gat uttered a curse that rang around the room and which earned him a frown from his father, who commented, "In the presence of a dragon a dog will howl, but a brave man will remain silent."

"The back of an elephant can be broken," countered Fang Gat, shortly. "Let your eyes rest upon this photograph."

The old man looked and his breath stopped short. "It would seem that the followers of evil are grouped under one roof and many questions are now answered."

"Some answered and some posed. Now, Rayne, you can see why Chaing was so anxious to get this box."

Rayne nodded. "My government will be very pleased to get a copy of this. Since the negative is here, I suggest that we have more prints made in great secrecy."

"My third son who deals in such mysteries can produce the required copies," said Fang So. "It will be done within the hour. What else is there?"

There was a short memorandum which bore the mark of Chaing receipting a quantity of money that made Rayne gasp. "There went rifles and food for a regiment into a private pocket."

Fang So nodded silently and touched a folded page with a talon-like forefinger. "And this?"

Rayne opened it and caught the table for support. "The other is trash," he croaked. "This—" He brushed his hand over his eyes and sat down.

Fang Gat picked up the sheet and read.

It will doubtless be worth a greater reward to your Excellency to know the location and exact number of atom bombs that are at this moment not outside of your Excellency's power. They could be taken by a surprise attack, since the forces guarding them will not be expecting attack. This cache is one of many scattered about the world, the idea being that it would be impossible with their stockpile thus dispersed to be knocked out completely by retaliatory bombing. The idea, while plausible, has the weakness that therefore others have the knowledge of the location of these stockpiles. They are quite vulnerable as they are insufficiently guarded. I can furnish details regarding the location of three of these interesting spots upon receipt of assurances from your Excellency that the required remuneration will be forthcoming. Let me emphasize: *A single submarine with a small, carefully chosen force could win another war.*

Silence hung thickly in the room, to be broken by Fang Gat's "It is signed 'Kung Wee.' "

"Which name might mean anything or nothing," averred Fang So, stroking his starved moustaches.

"It means one thing," said Rayne getting to his feet. "There isn't a minute to lose tracing this thing down. If this is common knowledge, the mind locks up trying to anticipate the possibilities."

"Man," said Fang So sadly, "is the weakness of men. The noblest sentiment ever fledged always has a cur barking at its heels and striving to bring it to nothing."

"What will you do?" asked Fang Gat.

Rayne shrugged. "At the moment, all I can do is go to the American Consulate and send a coded cable to Washington. Then I will have done what I can, unless it is decided that I go further into this. What will you do?"

Fang Gat shrugged. "At the moment, the nebulous Kung Wee and less nebulous Chaing are not within reach of my government. I might suggest that one, maybe both, are within reach of yours."

Rayne nodded. "You may rest assured that they will be taken care of. You may give me a copy of the photograph and I suggest that you place the negative in a safe place until the proper persons in your government are informed. I should like to know the fate of the man who collected this material."

"He is doubtless with his ancestors," stated Fang So. "Nor do I envy him the method of his passing, since it is obvious that from his suffering lips they extracted every scrap of evidence he was able to provide. I can imagine the consternation that must still plague the beds of those upon whose conscience this matter rests. I marvel that the iniquitous Chaing could be so stupid as to think that you, an agent of your country which you had served well, would ever deliver to him a box of this value without looking inside."

Rayne shrugged. "I think he, like many orientals, has an entirely mistaken sense of Anglo-Saxon temperament —as the Japanese were mistaken in thinking that we wouldn't fight. Chaing was probably being quite clever in his own opinion when he chose me, thinking that since he is a 'patriot' and I an ex-agent, I would accept him at his stated value. He was also ill-advised to speak to his fellow in Cantonese, thinking that I did not understand the language. Stupidity cannot in some cases be explained. In a case like this it can, with all sincerity, be saluted."

Fang So chuckled silently. "A stupid man makes it easy for a man of ordinarily modest talents to be clever. I see you are eager to depart, my son. Go, with the blessing of an old man who admires your people and most especially the one with whom he has been seriously associated."

Rayne bowed before him. "Long life, venerable Fang So, and a thousand sons."

"To you long life, great happiness and children to grace your declining years. May numerous watchful gods guard every footstep you take in this world and may they take you by the hand in the next."

Fang Gat gripped his hand at the doorway. "Were this to be the last meeting I think I would be overcome with grief. Somehow I cannot believe that it will be."

"Nor I. But there is still a question unanswered that I should not ask. What will you do with Marlene? I know you have paid for her hotel room."

"Only pending the arrival of her substance from Macassar. She was shrewder than we thought. She didn't give it all to Moak. As to what I shall do, only the gods can tell. I think the heart might overcome face."

"See that it does. I should think that face would be cold comfort on a lonely night. So long, fella. I'll see you before you know it."

"Well," said Tom White, stroking the mane of his roan mare, "Amy 'lowed as to how you needed a woman."

"How did Amy take meeting a foreigner?" asked Rayne.

"Hell, Amy took to the gals like a duck to com meal. Amy ain't no uppity-nosed woman. There'll be talk, o' course, but if any of it gits to her she'll burn it off right to the hide. Hi, Perc."

Perc reined his bay gelding to a stop. "Greetings, Tom. What do you think of our feeding pen?"

" 'Tain't got no northern cover. Wind'll blow through them slats like a fire goin' through weeds."

"We intend to hay that up good and thick before winter," said Rayne.

"Well, got to make a move," said Tom, sitting straight in his saddle. "Got some lambs to dock this evenin'. Y'all come over any chanct you git and we'll open a keg o' nails." He touched the roan with a spur and trotted away toward the woods.

"Well, now," said Perc in astonishment. "What do you suppose he meant by opening a keg of nails? Going to carpenter or something?"

Rayne laughed. "That's local argot. It means beer or some drink will be opened."

Perc grimaced. "Rum, looks like I'll never catch on to this. And hell, they have just as much trouble trying to understand me." He breathed deeply. "Finest country in the world. And those *Santa Gertrudis* cattle are fine. Gad, how they grow! Beats sheep all hollow. Smelly nuisances, they are." He cut a glance at Rayne as they rode toward the house where Taneeta and Loa sat under the spreading pecan tree, clad in the skimpiest of shorts and halters. "There's one thing, Rayne. Dashed if I quite understand why you took us in here like you did —your own home and all that. Foreigners, both of us, you know."

Rayne skidded forward comfortably in his saddle. "It's not hard to explain, Perc. Seriously, I didn't want anything to change Loa. She came from the assembly line with everything there. Nothing missing."

"You mean in the crumpet?"

"There and elsewhere. I know she seduced you the first night aboard the *Lena* and she hasn't had a lick of trouble out of you since. There are any number of places where conditions and people would have squeezed her and forced her into a pattern or broken her spirit. Here it won't happen. There'll be some murmuring about our 'foreign wives,' but after a time they'll be accepted and admired because they're different."

Perc's face had flamed at the mention of the seduction. "Jolly helpless cove, I was. Didn't stand a chance and she knew it. And to think I had things to say about you and Taneeta. Rum. Never had a chance." He chuckled. "Still don't."

Loa stroked the firm round bulge of her stomach with a sort of rapt religious avidity.

"Why," she asked, "do you love your husband?"

Taneeta showed her white teeth in a replete smile. "Many reasons. One big one—the way he handled my father with words. My father found himself beaten by words, his own favorite weapon. Rayne simply blew him down with a broadside of pure logic, and then told him that we were legally married and there was nothing he could do about it."

Loa nodded and looked toward the two men as they rode toward the corral. "I love Perc because he is such a baby. He is mine and here is mine and his." She stroked her stomach again.

"Apart, we were only half a people. Together and here we are one complete people."

They pulled up at the corral gate and Rayne pointed to Loa and Taneeta. "Take a look at them. Happy and content. Boy, between us we have the two most delectable morsels of woman-flesh on this or any other continent."

Perc nodded and swallowed as he looked at the lengths of golden leg, bare smooth stomachs and swelling breasts. That Loa's stomach was a little larger than the minimum requirements of symmetry heightened his admiration and rekindled the feeling that it was all some sort of fantasy, some day to be revealed as a delusion and a vision of drunkenness.

"Rum," he said hoarsely. "Suppose I hadn't come into Voort's that day, just at the right time."

Rayne nodded. "Suppose Chaing had gone to some other operative that night, instead of me."

Perc grinned suddenly. "What say we bung around there and nibble a bit on our respective sweetmeats? Let's bung the horses into a stable first, what what?"

"Right jolly ho, and all that sort of supremely jolly old British-American chin-chin."

They both laughed together heartily.

THE END